Luke's Tale

A Story of Unconditional Love

By

Carol McKibben

TROLL RIVER PUBLICATIONS
LOS ANGELES, CA

Troll River Publications

www.trollriverpub.com

Luke's Tale:
A Story of Unconditional Love

ISBN: 978-1-939564-02-3

For information, contact Troll River Publications: www.trollriverpub.com

DEDICATION

For Luke, Leia, Darth, Yoda, Tipper and Simon – My inspiration.
And to Mark, Debi, Lauren and Stephanie – whose encouragement
made it all possible.

If we make our goal to live a life of compassion and unconditional love, then the world will indeed become a garden where all kinds of flowers can bloom and grow.

- Dr. Elisabeth Kübler-Ross, Late Author of *On Death and Dying*

Prologue

September 15, 2015

The world is darker today. Not because I'm blind. My world is always black. But this day my heart is broken.

I sit for a very long time next to the door. I long for her smell of fresh cut flowers, her touch and her gentle voice. I visualize her face. I see the fullness of her lips and the deep compassion in her dark eyes. She is the most caring human I've ever known. I long for her comforting arms around me.

People come up and pet me. One nurse offers me a bowl of water. I remain aloof, not wanting to be distracted in case… in case there's some word. She couldn't possibly be capable of being with me now.

Bay leaf and ocean scent assault my nostrils as I feel Ashlundt pass by into the ER. I stretch my nose toward him, searching for some sort of hope. I feel his desperation as he hurries past me with two words, "Stay, Luke."

My stomach growls. I suppress the hunger. It doesn't matter now. In trying to push away the anguish, my mind wanders back to when Sara left us. I was younger and not blind. She wanted to protect Ashlundt from the pain of her cancer. She must have known that he wouldn't be able to cope with her being sick.

I'm not sure what makes him tick. It has to have something to do with his brother's surfing accident. He blames himself to this day. Maybe that's why he can't cope with illness or imperfection in those he's supposed to love. I once was his golden boy. We went everywhere together. Now, my blindness has pushed him further away from me.

I still feel Ashlundt's athletic strength every once in a while. He'll brush his large hands over me, and I can visualize his big frame and angular face bathed in his long, sun-lightened hair. I wish he knew how to cope with my blindness. It's hard not to take it personally.

I wish I could cope better with my loss of sight. I'd always been a watcher. It must be part of my Lab nature. What scares me the most is that I can't observe my humans, or help them now. Sara has always depended upon our unspoken bond. Ashlundt is another story. I've been through tough times with each of them, and I've had to be more like that human detective, Sherlock Holmes, than a dog for them. I am the product of a broken relationship.

It's long past my evening meal when I feel Sara's presence. I hear nothing but the despair in her voice. "Come, Luke." She takes me by the collar and leads me to the car.

I sit in the backseat and slowly lie down. I know what has happened but can't bear thinking of it. She is silent, but her pain is unbearable and palpable in the air. I think back to how Ashlundt pushed her away, even when he finally discovered she was sick. I fought so hard to help him try and win her back…

I'm jarred back to reality as the car stops. I hear the door open, then the backseat door. Sara whispers, "Let's go inside, Luke."

Slowly, I follow Sara into the house.

She says nothing as she fixes my kibble and leftover chicken, then leaves the room. My greatest fear has been realized.

After sating my hunger, I go to find Sara in her bedroom. She is lying across her bed in silence, tortured and bereft. Even though I'm not usually allowed on the bed, she says nothing as I crawl up next to her and place my head on her hip. I give out a whimpered cry of sorrow.

We lie together in silence for a long, long time. I have to go outside so badly that my bladder hurts, but I don't dare leave Sara. She is so cold. I move closer to her, wanting her to feel my warmth, the warmth that Ashlundt should have offered. Time passes. My stomach begins to growl and adds to my discomfort, but it doesn't matter. I will not leave her.

Sometime later the phone starts to ring. It must be morning. All those distraught voices leaving messages of sorrow on the answering machine. I crawl up to her face, pressing my nose on her cheek to see if she is asleep. Her hand softly touches the top of my head. "It's okay, Lukey. Thank you for staying with me." A ragged sigh escapes from her and is joined by my own.

Still we remain motionless. I think back to the chain of events before I started going blind. But, I've gotten way ahead of myself. I need to go back to the beginning so that you understand how we arrived at our darkest moment in time.

Luke's Tale

Chapter One

The Deception

June 24, 2010

Ashlundt Jaynes didn't know about the cancer, but I smelled it on Sara Colson from the beginning. I may just be a dog, but when she lied to him about it, I realized I had to help them.

I was born a large, blonde Labrador Retriever—a handsome, big-boned guy with a large square head and an unusually fine mind, so it was easy for me to reach the knobs and learn how to open doors… unless they were locked. Without too much exertion of my 87-pounds, I could just nudge them open with my nose and saunter in to be with my humans. They always seemed so pleased when I entered the room. Well, all except for this one time when I wandered into the master bathroom on that fateful day to find Sara, with her long dark hair tangled around her face, hunched over the edge of the bathtub crying.

I have to emphasize that I truly understand humans. I took great pride in my ability to comprehend the events surrounding me.

Since my birth, I had never seen Sara cry. It startled me. I plodded over to lick her face and hands, trying to wipe the tears away. She grabbed my head, slid to the marble tile floor and buried her face in my furry neck.

"Oh, Luke, what am I gonna do? I can't add my problems to his," she moaned.

I whined in Sara's ear and plopped down next to her with my head in her lap. She cupped her arms around her left breast and rocked back and forth. "Your mommy needs an operation. Chemo too." She rubbed the top of my head. "Ash can't deal with me being sick." Sara bent down and rested her cheek on my ear. "With the lawsuit and all this would be… too much. I need to go away for a while…" Her voice trailed off.

I pressed my nose closer to her mouth and smelled the disease on her breath. A dog's olfactory senses are much greater than a human's, or so I've overheard. I knew it was bad. It was very much like the last time I saw our old next door neighbor, Mrs. Simmons. She patted me on the head in front of her house one afternoon. She was so weak and sluggish. It was like all her strength had been taken away. A week later, the ambulance was taking her away for the last time. Now, as Sara held me tighter, my body began to tremble with hers at the fear of losing her.

****

Sara moved through the house like an invisible stranger, not her usual demeanor. She was lithe or "gracefully athletic" as Ashlundt phrased it. She didn't just walk into a room; she dominated it. But after our moment in the bathroom, she seemed to dissolve. I dogged behind her as much as she would let me. She wandered listlessly through our one-story ranch-style house, from the large open kitchen with its brick floors, to the adjoining den with its stone fireplace.

The house was filled with hard-surfaced textures that Sara had softened with earth-tone fabric, pillows, flowers and Southwestern-styled rugs. I'd track her into her home office, once a bedroom with an adjoining bathroom. She'd sit for a while, then get up and shuffle into their master bedroom across the hall and start folding towels and putting them away in the closet. It almost became a routine. She'd walk to the large waveless waterbed and stretch out on the delicious chenille bedspread that I wanted to snuggle into with her. After a few minutes, she'd get up and slowly saunter by Ashlundt's office, a converted rec room at the end of the house next to the garage. She would pause for a minute, glance in, then shuffle to her bathroom where she would lock herself in for long periods of time. She had always kept the doors unlocked so I could join her in any room. Now, I was resigned to just waiting.

Our long walks on the horse paths in the woods surrounding our house were always the favorite part of my day.

2

Weather took on a significant essence in the woods – full of the fragrance of the pine and oak trees in summer, or the crunch of the path on cooler days. Only at that point, everything was overcast and gray with Sara deep in thought, lying across a fallen log on a trail. And, again, I waited. It never used to be like this.

Ashlundt didn't notice. Once, after Sara had locked herself in the bathroom too many times, I went into his home office and peeked up over his wooden desk. He sat in his high-backed, black leather chair, his shoulder-length blonde hair falling around his unshaven face as he stared blankly at his desk. Tell-tale signs of many sleepless nights were etched across his face. His tall frame was hunched over a book. In a t-shirt and shorts, he looked more like the surfer-dude in the framed photos on the wall behind his desk than a respected psychologist. Suddenly, he looked up and fixed me with his steel blue eyes that used to always be filled with laughter. "Damn, Luke!" He quickly picked up the book and hurled it to the floor.

It hurt me to see how an unfair lawsuit had reduced this vibrant, kind man, who was always full of fun, into this angry shadow of himself. The steady decline of patients that visited him (and generously brought me treats) had fallen to an all-time low. Half his built-in oak bookshelves were empty. His office floor was littered with haphazard piles of books he had hoisted there in anger. He was often distracted at the dinner table. *Odd behavior for a psychologist,* I thought. It was so unlike what I had always known of him. Boyish, charming and handsome, with a strong chin and broad shoulders, his blue eyes usually sparkled with mischief when he looked at Sara and me.

Ashlundt was a casual man. Our life together had always been relaxed... 'til now. Growing up in San Diego, his entire family was into surfing. I heard Sara once say that Ashlundt had been a champion; that he almost went on the professional circuit before deciding to go to college. I knew he had a large family, but in the year I had been with him they had only visited us once. And another time, we had gone to their beach house in San Diego where they all showed off their surf board skills. Sara and I were thoroughly entertained. They all had unusual first names that started with an "A" ... Ashlundt, Asa, Anya, Ardin and Asmara. Of course, Ashlundt was my favorite of the "A" group. Although I also really enjoyed Asmara, the youngest of the three boys. Asa and Anya were the parents.

A few days after Sara revealed her cancer to me, I watched as she peeked around Ashlundt's office door and entered with a question. "Hey, you think we could we go out for dinner and a movie tonight?"

"Sara, I just don't feel up to it. Sorry," Ashlundt seemed to be lost in thought. He didn't look up, but instead kept his eyes fixed on the papers on his desk.

Sara took a tentative step into the office. "Well, how 'bout if we take Luke for a walk to the equestrian center after dinner? You know, just spend time together?"

I seconded that with a large "Ruff!"

Ashlundt sat back rubbing his arm across his forehead. He sighed. "I'm really sorry. Have to finish this marketing plan!" The frustration rose in his voice.

I watched her melt away back into her office at the opposite end of the hall. I followed her, attempted to get into her lap and lick her face -- only to be pushed away. I was momentarily shocked. Sara had never refused my affection. I pushed on and offered to play ball and Frisbee, bringing them each to her and dropping them at her feet. Her reaction: "Stop it, Luke! Go lie down!" I couldn't believe what I was hearing but persisted, placing my chin on her knees and letting out a deep sigh. She looked down at me, melted and wrapped her arms around my neck.

I knew she was thinking about that awful illness, and she confirmed it with her next words.

"I love him too much to put him through the pain of my illness." She rubbed my snout, and I licked her hand. "He's been destroyed by the malpractice suit."

I sympathized by whining and licking her hand harder.

"And then there's his brother."

I was puzzled by that. *Which brother*?

"It'll be easier for him if he thinks I'm away for other reasons…"

She trailed off and started to cry again. I licked her face, but she sobbed harder. I backed away and pondered what to do. I knew she was trying to protect Ashlundt, but this was wrong. I had to force her to tell him. So, I padded down the hall from her office to his, took his t-shirt in between my teeth and tugged. This was my attempt to get him to follow me to her. He was in the middle of a phone call and pushed me away. At the same time, he covered the mouthpiece. "Stop it," he commanded and glared at me.

I sat back on my haunches and waited until he hung up. Then, I tried again. I placed a large paw on his leg and whined.

His face suddenly softened, and kindness flooded into his eyes. "What is it, Luke? You okay, boy?"

I barked and wagged my tail, then turned and ran to the door. I stopped and cocked my head at him. He shook his head from side-to-side. "Sorry, boy. Can't play with you now. Gotta work."

Again, I walked up to him and barked loudly several times. "Ruff! Ruff!" This seemed to grab his attention.

"Oh, all right, I'll throw the Frisbee for a few minutes." He laughed as he jumped out of his leather high-back chair and followed me. The in-his-face loud barking routine always seemed to work with him. It was my go-to move.

I ran straight into Sara's office. She was sitting at her desk, her head slumped down in her hands. She was still crying. Ashlundt rushed to her side. "Sara, what's the matter? What's happened?" He knelt beside her chair and put his arms around her.

"No-nothing," she stuttered and flashed me a look I couldn't decipher.

"Then, why are you crying?"

Sara's nose was all red and irritated. She blew it into a tissue, crumpled it in her hand and took a deep breath. "I just have some decisions to make right now; that's all."

"Decisions? About what?" Ashlundt stared at her, eyebrows arched.

"Well, I got a job offer," she softly replied. She turned her eyes downward as she said this. Sara didn't lie often, but I could sense the few times when she did. Ashlundt seemed oblivious.

"Really, that's great! Where?"

She paused, then whispered, "In England."

"England? As in across the ocean?" His mouth hung wide open in complete surprise.

"Yes, at Oxford… as a… teaching assistant. I'll be able to do my research. Uh… my book has received some good reviews… and they called me," she lied on and shifted nervously in her chair.

I growled at her. She shot me a sharp warning glance.

"When did this happen?" Ashlundt threw his hands upward in disgust and stood looking down at her. "You haven't said a word to me. Why would you consider it without talking to me?"

"That's why I wanted to go to dinner with you. You've been so preoccupied since the lawsuit, and… and I have to think about my career; my future. Maybe I can get my psychology doctorate; be on a level footing with you. It's just for a year." She straightened from her slumped position in her desk chair and looked up at him. "We've been together for awhile now… and… well… I haven't been one of your recent priorities."

He looked at her with a furrowed brow. "Priorities? Have you not been aware of what I've gone through? I was raked over the coals for something I didn't do. And it's all but destroyed my practice." He let out a huge breath and walked in a circle, frantically running his hands through his hair. "That girl's suicide, it wasn't my fault, no matter what charges her father brought against me. I've been fighting to rebuild our lives," he shot back at her. His face grew redder with each syllable. Now keep in mind, I couldn't see colors, but, honestly, I could see the discoloration in humans' faces and knew that meant they were turning red.

"Our lives?" she snorted now getting angry. "Our lives? YOUR life. You say you love me but we've been so… disconnected."

"Oh, you mean marriage. We're talking about marriage here! Ashlundt squinted and stared sharply into her face. "Sara, I've told you how many times that I want to marry you. But I'm just trying to work things out financially for us. The last thing we need to do now is try and make a big wedding."

I sat just behind them and followed their retorts like a tennis match, my head swiveling from one to the other. I wanted to scream at them to stop.

She gasped. "I didn't mean that! But, is it that repugnant to you, Ash?" Sara slapped her hand on her knee to emphasize the point. I recoiled in momentary fear.

"Of course not! You're being unreasonable now. Why? Why are you doing this? Do you wanna leave me and go to England?" He raised his voice and threw up his arms. "Is that it?"

She shot up, tears rolling down her face. With a defiant "Yes," she ran from the room. Ashlundt stood staring at her empty chair with his mouth hanging open.

I just made it inside the master bathroom across the hall, my toenails clawing at the polished wood floors, before she slammed the door. Sara crumbled to her knees next to the bathtub, her fingers twisting at a ragged hole above the knee in her jeans. "Luke, I had to lie to him." Then, more to herself than me, she mumbled, "He needs time to heal; doesn't need me as a distraction right now."

I lay down next to her with my head in her lap and tried to comfort her as best I could. *Didn't she see that Ashlundt wasn't himself right now? Couldn't she offer him the truth about her illness so he could maybe help her? Did she think he wouldn't love her if he knew she was sick? Why did she want to make him think that she didn't want to be with him? Wouldn't that hurt him more? Ashlundt had to stop her from leaving. She had to tell him the truth.*

****

Several days of arguing between Sara and Ashlundt were torturous on my sensitive ears. Then, Sara started packing. She began to put individual pieces of clothing in plastic bags and arranged them in her suitcase. Ashlundt kept a watchful eye in their bedroom.

"Hey, it's just for a year and then I come back. It's for the best. Without me here, you can focus on rebuilding the business. You won't have pressure to entertain me, or… plan our wedding." She opened her jewelry box on the dresser as if to take something from it, then suddenly shut it.

"But, I want you here. And how can you leave Luke for an entire year? We'll both be so lonely without you." His hands pushed deep into his khaki pants, he paced back and forth like a dejected schoolboy alongside the bed where her suitcase was being stuffed.

She sighed, then took a deep breath while turning to him. "Oh, Luke. Of course I'll miss him! But I know you'll take the best of care." She picked up an orange summer skirt and placed it in another plastic bag. "And hey, it'll be over before you know it. By then I'll have hopefully made a giant leap in my career. Who knows? Maybe we'll be able to have a practice together some day."

I was frantic. I ran back and forth between the two of them. I tried to will Sara not to leave. It was hopeless. She somehow couldn't understand that real love means loving someone no matter what. Or at least, that's how I saw love. My people were everything to me. I would love Sara no matter what happened. It was how my brain was wired. That was what I heard her friends say about her book; she was supposed to be the expert on unconditional love. Love really did make humans oblivious.

She snapped shut her last bag and bent down and wrapped her arms around me. "I love you, Lukey. Don't forget me, boy." I covered her face with kisses, then rolled over on my back hoping to con her into a belly rub. Just maybe my irresistible appeal would change her mind. *No such luck.* She gave my head a last pat and stood to face Ashlundt.

"Please, Sara. Please don't leave me." He placed his hands together in a pleading gesture. "You're the only one who can put up with me. You know how to make me smile. You always know what I need. How can I go on without you here?"

If I spoke in human words, mine would have echoed those that Ashlundt had just uttered. His pleas brought back memories of the day he'd been hit with the lawsuit; how he had gone into a dark funk smoldering in his office. I recalled Sara sitting in his lap, holding him close and kissing his face. Words weren't necessary. Soon, she took him by the hand and led him to the backyard where the delicious aroma of barbecued steaks assaulted our senses. As he took in the aroma, she handed him a gift.

"Sara, what's this?"

"Open it, silly!"

Ripping the paper away, he held a frame in his hand. "It's *Hagar the Horrible*! I love this comic strip, Sara."

"Remember, Ash, 'Don't sweat the small stuff, and it's all small stuff! That's the moral of the story."

Then, she started with her silly lawyer jokes. "How do you know when a lawyer is lying? . . . His lips are moving. *"*

Ashlundt broke a smile with that one.

"What do lawyers use for birth control? . . . Their personalities!" They both broke into hysterics. I hunkered down on a slab of beef Sara had tossed my way.

Ashlundt's voice jogged me back to the reality that she was leaving us. "Please don't do this, Sara!"

She picked up her bags, and we followed her to the driveway in the front yard.

"Sara, I love you. Please don't do this!"

His plea made Sara hesitate for a moment. Her thin arms trembled even in the warmth of the June day. She stared at him, then reached out and pushed a lock of blonde hair from his forehead. "You'll be fine. I'll send you my contact info as soon as I get settled. In the meantime, my cell phone should work."

His response was to grab and enfold her in his arms. "I love you, and we will get married as soon as you get back." He pushed her away at arms length and looked at her with fear in his eyes, "Promise me you'll come back?"

"Of... of course, Ash..." Her voice trailed off.

I knew that she had to be unsure if she would beat the cancer. How could she know if she would make it back? I replayed the picture of Mrs. Simmons being put in the ambulance over and over, and my heart ached for her.

Ashlundt wrapped his arms around her one last time. "You better, no matter what."

She turned quickly and stuffed her luggage into the back of her car. And then... she was gone.

We stood in the fenced front yard and watched the little blue and white Mini Cooper back out of the driveway. It was the one that Ashlundt had given her for her 23rd birthday. Soon, it rounded the turn and disappeared. Ashlundt dropped to the grass with me and wrapped his arms around me. I smothered him with a wet nose and pressed against him to let him know I was there for him. I loved them both, no matter what, and I knew that it was important for me to somehow get them back together. I just didn't know how. Not then, anyway.

Luke's Tale

Chapter Two

The Beginning

Ashlundt and I sat in the grass for a while. I thought about trying to get him to chase me through the two-acres of land surrounding our house in Bell Canyon. After all, it was early summer and the grass smelled so good. I nudged him and wagged my tail, but he patted my head and said nothing. I thought about why I loved him, even when he was a grump. He wasn't usually so self-absorbed. I was his friend and confidant, just as I was for Sara. I went everywhere with him. I would even lie on my doggie bed in his office during his client sessions. And afterward, he would record his thoughts and talk through cases with me. I loved the compassion that he showed for each one of them.

One such session was about a housewife with a serious addiction. After she left, Ashlundt sat in his consultation chair with a mug of coffee, writing his notes. He carried on the usual one-sided conversation with me. "Poor Mrs. Hall; she's in such denial about those painkillers. She's convinced herself that she's still in physical pain. What she's really doing is escaping the pain of the past patterns she's brought into the present. I don't want to be tough on her, but I think I have to be to make her face it."

He was boyish and charming when he wasn't depressed. He often surprised Sara and me with unexpected gifts. Whenever he brought her a present, he would give me one as well. I particularly liked the hard rubber balls that I could chase after, or the fluffy stuffed toys I carried around in my mouth endlessly. My favorite was a Teddy Bear he had given me when I was old enough not to just immediately rip its poor eyes and nose off. Luckily, it was only missing one eye and part of its left ear that Sara had sewn shut to prevent me from strewing stuffing all over the house.

To celebrate our first year together, he took us to a dog-friendly outdoor café near Santa Barbara. It was on the Pacific Ocean, and the menu not only included specials for children, but items for canines too. After snarfing down an order of boneless chicken breasts, I looked on as Ashlundt reached across his T-bone steak – from which he promised me a good chew later – and took Sara's hands. "Do you have any idea how much I love you?"

"Hmm… maybe half as much as I adore you?" She teased.

Laughing, he said, "It's been a year since you moved in, and there's no happier man than me. I have you and Luke and the whole world ahead of us."

Before Sara could respond, and, as if on cue, the waitress served two velvet boxes on a tray. "Ash, what's this?"

"A token of my affection," he smiled as he pushed the two boxes toward her. She reached for the smaller box first and uncovered a silver bracelet with doggie charms. Snatching it from her hand, Ashlundt jumped up from his chair and snapped the shining adornment on her wrist. Then, unable to contain himself while Sara admired her new treasure, he opened the larger box and pulled out a matching collar for me.

Sara squealed and leaped into his arms. "Matching jewelry for Lukey and me!"

After she had smothered his face with kisses, he turned and removed my old collar, which was beginning to get a bit tight in the neck. The new one felt so much more secure and yet loose at the same time. It was perfect. In gratitude, I licked his hand and gave a soft bark of thanks. *I was quite the stylish guy.*

After dinner, we walked on the beach. I chased my favorite pink and green floppy Frisbee, a bit chewed up but still displaying a happy PetCo logo. But the best part was how affectionate they were with each other. When he took her in his arms and kissed her, I took off running down the beach, barking for joy. I like affection. What dog or human doesn't?

Tim Benson from across the street interrupted my daydream when he yelled over to us sitting on the front lawn. "Ash, come over; have a beer with me. Corky just made some biscuits and sausage."

That invite got my attention. If anything could distract me from the sadness of Sara's abrupt departure, it would be grilled meat. I nudged Ashlundt, then ran to the gate.

"Sounds good, Tim," Ashlundt yelled back.

"Bring Sara and Luke," Tim urged. Ashlundt jumped up, and we walked directly across the wide one-lane street and around their two-story brick house to the back patio that the Bensons inhabited on the weekends. "Sara's not here right now." Ashlundt offered no other explanation. I assumed he felt too raw to talk about her departure.

I loved Tim and Corky. Their house was like a second home to me, and I often hung out with them when Ashlundt and Sara went out at night. Tim was really tall, like Ashlundt. He kept his big frame in shape by playing in a men's basketball league and working out at the gym. He was completely bald and wore glasses with no frames. A quiet man, he was not one for small talk but was sincere when he spoke. His wife Corky was a favorite of mine. She always fed me! About a foot and a half shorter than her husband, she was a shapely woman with large bones and an easy laugh, despite the pain from arthritic hips that plagued her. Maybe it's because she was older, but she had a way of fixing her dark brown eyes on people as if she could see through them.

"Well, pull up a chair," Corky said as she handed him a bottle of Molson and a plate of sausage and biscuits. I felt the drool streaming from my mouth and onto their stone patio floor. Without another word, she set a plate of sausages cut into nice bite sizes down next to me.

"He really shouldn't eat those, Corky," Ashlundt cautioned.

"Oh, for heaven's sake, let the poor creature enjoy himself," Corky, a devout foodie, quipped. That was all the permission I needed before devouring the meat in a mouthful of bites. As if I was going to wait for permission to eat the food lying in front of me?

Tim and Corky Benson had become my humans' good friends. They often got together to play Bridge or watch movies on the Benson's big screen television. I was always invited and got to share a large bowl of popcorn. Corky was a sucker for my desperate, pleading eyes.

"So, Ash," Corky said as she sat down in a lawn chair next to him, "you never told me the story about how you and Sara met. All this time, and I've never gotten around to asking you. But…… she's not here now, so give with it." She laughed.

Lousy timing, Corky, I thought to myself.

Ashlundt seemed reluctant at first. "You mean Sara hasn't filled you in? You've known her a couple of years now."

"You know, I never see her without you around," Corky replied. "Just never had the chance to ask, I guess. Besides, I wanna hear *your* version."

"You know women," Tim interjected. "So nosey." He ducked as Corky threw a pillow from one of the patio chairs in his general direction. It landed a few inches from my hind paws.

Everyone laughed, and Ashundt seemed to relax and open up. "Well, Corky, this will probably sound all mushy, but I loved her from the moment I saw her." He waited for Corky to finish her "awwww" before going forward. "So anyway, I had taken old Bear in to Dr. Wild for another round of chemo, and there she sat re-filing folders and handling other patients. I hadn't seen her there before."

My predecessor Bear, according to Ashlundt, had been a large black lab that he'd had for about 13 years before he passed away. He'd gotten him when he was still a teenager.

"Bear. He was such a great dog," Corky murmured.

Ashlundt shrugged and smiled. "Yes, he was special."

"I remember those chemo days. It was amazing how well he withstood them." She paused for a few minutes, then leaned toward Ashlundt and urged him on, "What happened next? Don't spare any details."

Ashlundt stretched his legs out in front of him and took a long sip of his beer. "It wasn't so much what happened but how I *felt* as I walked toward her. When I reached the counter, she stood to lean over and scratch Bear's head. The lilt of her voice when she spoke to him, it made me lose my breath for a moment. I felt all dizzy and lightheaded like my universe had *shifted.* I remember thinking how tall she was…you know she's just four inches shorter than me. And she just looked straight into my eyes, like she could read my thoughts."

"Wow! That really does sound like love at first sight. So what did *you* say?" Corky leaned forward even more, her chin resting on her cupped hands.

Ashlundt grinned full of mischief. "She spoke first. She looked up at me and said, "You must be Dr. Jaynes.""

"No Ash, get past all that stuff… you know what I mean! Get to the good part." Corky sounded insistent. Tim interjected again with, "Give the doc a break."

"No, it's okay, Tim." Ashlundt smiled sheepishly. "I remember saying, 'Ashlundt. Call me Ash.' And then I said, 'This is Bear. He's here for his chemo.' And then I thought, 'She knows that already, stupid.'"

"I think she knew that I was embarrassed because she just smiled and took Bear's leash to take him back for his blood test, and when she did, I purposely touched her hand. An electric spark shocked us. 'Must be the crazy weather we're having,' she said with this funny look on her face." Ashlundt turned up his beer and gulped the remainder down.

"Want another beer?" Tim was holding out another bottle of Molson.

"Yeah, have another round," Corky insisted. "I wanna hear more."

I got up and stretched, then moved closer to Ashlundt's chair. He was totally into the story now.

"Sure, I'd love another. Guess I'm pretty thirsty." He reached out for the beer, then settled back in his chair. "Where was I. Oh, I took a seat and started plotting how I could ask her out and not seem like a player, or anything. When she was back behind the desk, I noticed that the lobby had emptied out. So, I took the opportunity to find out more about her. I asked if she was new at the clinic. She told me she was a huge dog lover and the job gave her a chance to help them." Ashlundt reached down and patted my head. "As it turns out, she'd started two weeks before to help pay the bills. She was trying to finish her graduate degree in psych at USC."

Even though I'd heard this story many times before, I still enjoyed hearing Ashlundt tell it. I inched closer to him and rested my head at his feet.

Ashlundt continued. "I told her it was a small world, and that I was a psychologist. She told me no way did I look like any of the psych majors that she knew. She said I looked more like a football player, and I told her that surfing was actually my sport."

Ashlundt always seemed embarrassed about his size. He ran his hands through his long, blonde hair and took a deep breath. "I think I was wearing shorts, one of my favorite Billabong t-shirts and flip flops. You know, my usual. Growing up with a big family on the ocean in San Diego, it tends to lend itself to casual wear! She asked me if I always dressed like that for the office. I told her it depended upon the client. Besides, no point in dressing up on Bear's chemo days."

Ashlundt seemed to be reveling in his memory of how he had met Sara. He didn't have to be asked to continue on, but I licked his toes and the flip flop on his right foot to encourage him.

"Anyhow, at some point, I told her if she'd ever like to talk with a practicing psychologist, or if I could help her with anything, that I'd be happy to oblige. Something professional like that. I gave her my card. And then she said the damnedest thing."

"What?" This time it was Tim who leaned forward and asked. "What'd she tell you?"

"She said: I think that would be terrific. How about my place tonight, eight o'clock for dinner? You bring Bear, of course, and the pizza. She winked when she took my card and handed me her address and phone number already written on a Post-It. I was so flabbergasted that all I could do was mutter: Well, I'll be damned."

"And how did the date go that night?" Corky's eyebrows elevated even higher.

Ashlundt chuckled. "It took us about half-way through the pizza to realize that we were both completely into each other. I spent the next two weeks bringing over take-out and just staring at her while she studied. She'd ask my opinion about various assignments, and Bear got quite comfortable on her old leather sofa. I started sleeping over at the end of the second week. A few months later, she gave up her apartment in Chatsworth and moved in with me here."

"Yeah, I remember that we lost old Bear just right after she first moved here with you," Tim said. "That was really a downer. Great, friendly guy he was."

I nudged Ashlundt and wagged my tail in salute to my fallen predecessor. Ashlundt sat forward and massaged the back of my ears in response. "Yep, that was pretty devastating for me. Bear was a gift from my... brother." Ashlundt shifted uncomfortably in his lounge chair.

"Which brother?" Corky asked.

"A younger brother, Aaron... You remember. The one that had the surfing accident with me... he... I tried to save him... got to him too late..."

I watched Ashlundt intently. This was something that I didn't know about him. I could see that he was getting agitated, and I worried that I didn't know more. I licked the leg nearest to me this time and tried to show my concern.

"Ash, I'm so sorry for bringing up a bad memory; forgive me." Corky shrugged in embarrassment. "Tim's right. I'm too nosey sometimes."

"No, it's all right, Corky. My family and I, we thought he'd make it, but he was in a coma... on a ventilator in the hospital for... a long time. I've never gotten over it." Ashlundt pushed his hair away from his face and took a quick sip of his beer. He stared at the ground for a moment lost in thought. "Watching my brother, then Bear struggle to live... I felt so helpless to change anything. That's the hardest part for me. Makes me angry."

"I don't think we ever get over losing the people, or the animals, that we love, Ash," Tim said and grabbed another serving of biscuit and sausage for his friend. I watched longingly as Ashlundt took the plate.

"But now you have beautiful Luke." Corky smiled, then leaned over and turned me over on my back. Her soft hands on my pink belly felt marvelous. *Such a kind and thoughtful woman.* She looked back up at Ashlundt and pressed on. "So, tell me about how you got Luke. We were gone on vacation when you got him. He was such an adorable pup; just never thought to ask."

"I think it was three months after we lost Bear. Man, I was moping around the house – seemed so empty without him. It was right before my 30th birthday." He bit into a sausage biscuit and

17

took a swig of his beer. "The whole thing was Sara's scheme. She planned us a day where we just happened to be right up the road from this breeder who just *happened* to have several eight-week old puppies for sale. Pretty clever, eh?"

Corky laughed. "Good ol' Sara. Never underestimate that woman's intelligence." Tim nodded in agreement.

"So listen, we got up that Saturday morning, and she suggested this out-of-the-blue drive to a farmer's market in Somis. It was conveniently located right across the road from a sign for Brown's Labs." Ashlundt again sipped his beer and took a bite of sausage chewing thoughtfully. "After we did our shopping, Sara was like: Oh, look, Ash, a lab breeder; can we go look, please?" Ashlundt laughed. "It was too funny. I think I told her 'no,' and she said something like: Come on, sour puss; the best way to heal the pain is to look at new puppies!"

"Weren't you starting to get suspicious?" Tim leaned back in his chair and crossed his long legs.

"Well, yeah. But, of course, we fell in love with Luke and brought him home." He reached down for me and scratched behind my ears. "Have to admit: he was the best medicine in the world for me. So strong and healthy. It's such a relief to know that I won't have to worry about him needing constant care. He's just the best buddy around."

His words made me perk up. I had to assume that Sara knew about Ashlundt's brother and how he felt about people being sick and helpless. *Perhaps she knew he wouldn't be able to deal well with her being sick?* That had to be the real reason why she just disappeared from us.

But how to get her back? That was my next challenge.

Chapter Three

The Discovery

At first he wasn't alarmed when he didn't hear from her. He sat in his office and talked aloud to me. "Why wouldn't she let me take her to the airport?" He fiddled with a paperweight on his desk. "What's she gonna do with her car? Why didn't I think of any of *that?*"

After six evening meals – my time was determined by my regular feedings – Ashlundt started to worry. "She should be there by now. Why hasn't she called me?" He looked at me like he expected an answer and dished out my regular kibble mixed with leftover beef stew. I gobbled down my meal, then followed him into his office where he dialed her cell phone. "Damn, voice mail," Ashlundt muttered.

Sara's parents had been killed in a car accident when she was 19, and she was an only child. I heard her explain why holidays sometimes made her sad to Corky once. She really was alone in the world but for her life with us and her friends. I was worried about her to begin with, but Ashlundt's nervousness made me want to scratch an itch I didn't have.

The next day, Ashlundt sat brooding at the small oak kitchen table. He was drinking his coffee in one of Sara's USC college mugs. I was just beginning to take my morning after-breakfast nap when he sprang up and ran to Sara's office. Startled, I padded after him, then sat and watched as he dug through Sara's desk drawers. "Where's her phone numbers?"

Papers made circles in the air before landing in a pile on the floor. "Bingo, Luke! It's her address book!" He found it at the very bottom of a bunch of files. Clutching it to his chest like a precious treasure, he carried it into his office, settled at his desk and began dialing the numbers of Sara's friends. I followed, then stretched out on my office bed in the corner of the room. His first message was to her best friend and old roommate, Debi.

"Hi, this is Ash. Please call me if you've talked to Sara in the last week or two. Thanks."

He tried her other good friends from USC, Lauren and Stephanie, and their mutual close buddy, Bruce Hines, Ashlundt's old college roommate. I had heard that Bruce was an oncologist and researcher –whatever that was - at the UCLA cancer clinic. After he had introduced Dr. Hines and Sara, they too had become good friends. Sara had often talked to Bruce about doing therapy with cancer patients. Ashlundt ended up leaving voice messages for all of them.

A call to Sara's former boss, Dr. Suzi Wild, left him with zip. "Hi, Ash. How's Sara doing at Oxford?"

"Haven't you talked to her?" was his quick response.

"No, other than when she gave her two weeks' notice at work. She told me about Oxford. What an exciting opportunity for her. Is there something wrong, Ash?"

"No, Suzi, nothing. I… she… it's just been a while since we talked," he tried to wash over the truth.

"Well, when you talk to her tell her I send my best."

"I will, Suzi, thanks."

He turned to me quickly, "Well, that was a wash out."

The phone calls went on for many days. Finding no success, Ashlundt decided to change his strategy. "Gonna block my phone number, boy. They've gotta be avoiding me 'coz they know it's me calling."

A call to the phone company seemed to resolve the caller id problem. But, he still waited until night this time before making his round of phone calls to Sara's friends. As always, he used his speaker phone.

"Debi. Hi! This is Ash. Quick question: Have you spoken to Sara in the last month?"

"Ash, hi, spoken to Sara? No, why?"

Ah, a live voice at the other end, not a beeping answering machine. Ash was probably right about blocking his number. I listened as he talked to Sara's friend.

"So she didn't tell you she was going to Oxford?" His face reflected his amazement.

"Oxford? Really, wow. That's cool. Good for her."

Ashlundt hunched closer to the speaker phone. "Debs, come on. She didn't tell you about it?"

"Uh, no. Haven't talked to her in a while. I must be out of the loop."

Ashlundt scratched his chin; his eyes filled with suspicion. "How can that be? She's one of your best friends?"

"Can't answer that, Ash."

Her voice was too cavalier, and that made me suspicious. I gave out a muffled growl, though Deb probably didn't hear me from her end.

"Ash, haven't you talked to her? I mean, you do live with her. If anyone would know anything…" Her voice tailed off.

"That's the whole point!" I could see his frustration growing. His face was reddening. He bit his lip and tried to dial down his temper. He squeezed his eyes shut as if in deep thought. "I'm just… she just… it's all a bit confusing. I thought maybe you could help." He rested his elbows on his knees, cupped his face with his hands and frowned still with his eyes shut.

"Look, Ash. I'll let you know if I hear from her. All right?"

"Sure, thanks. I'd appreciate it." He hit the off button on the phone, stood up, grabbed a book from his desk and pitched it against the wall. "Damn! She's clueless, Luke."

I stood up from my bed and barked once in agreement. Ash patted me on the head, then sat back down in his chair, hit the speaker button on his phone and dialed another number.

"Bruce, it's Ash. Got a minute?"

"Hey, Ash. What's up?"

"What's up? Well, for starters, why the hell haven't you returned my calls?" Ashlundt kicked off his flip flops under the desk, stood up and began to pace.

"Sorry, man. I've been swamped. My caseload's insane these days. I've also been training some new residents. You know how it is."

"Okay, never mind. You got my messages... so, have you talked to Sara in the last month?" He stopped and shrugged, his hands pointed upward.

"Sara, no, why?" Hines' voice was cautious.

"She's over at Oxford. Went for a year as an assistant. Says she's completing her doctorate. But she isn't answering her cell. I can't get hold of her." Ashlundt walked back to his chair and plopped down hard into it. "Weird, eh?"

"Hmmm... well, you know cell phones can be dodgy in Europe, Ash."

"Voice mail works fine, Bruce! She's not calling me back. Something's wrong. Didn't Sara tell you she was going to Oxford?" Ashlundt was up and pacing again and on the point of losing it.

"Nope. Didn't know, but that's great news!"

"This isn't right! Debi didn't know either. You'd think this would be something she'd tell her best friends. Look, if you hear anything, call me ASAP, okay?"

"Of course, man. Calm down. I'm sure you'll hear from her. She loves you, Ash; you know that."

Ashlundt took a deep breath. He seemed to relax a little. "Okay, Bruce, thanks. Call me if you hear."

More calls to Sara's other girlfriends yielded the same results. They all sounded surprised to learn from him that she had gone to London.

When Ashlundt had finally checked off the last name on his list, he jumped up from his desk and started pacing back and forth between the kitchen and his office. I jumped up and followed him, my tail wagging the whole time. I was surely hoping for a late-night snack, but it didn't materialize. Instead, Ashlundt made a cup of coffee for himself and checked his watch. "Hmmm... after midnight here; should be morning there."

I followed him back into his office and watched him down the cup of coffee. For several minutes, he sat, drumming his fingers on his desk. Finally, he seemed to find his courage. "Luke, boy. I'm gonna call the psych department at Oxford. They'll tell me the truth." Slowly, he dialed the digits until a funny double ringing sound filled his speaker.

"Margaret Hyde-White," a woman's voice answered.

"Hello, this is Dr. Ashlundt Jaynes from Los Angeles. Are you the dean's assistant?"

"Yes sir. That would be me. And how can I assist you?"

"Um, well, I'm trying to locate a friend of mine, Sara Colson. She recently accepted a position in your department."

"Hold on. I'll call up her file on my computer, Dr. Jaynes."

Ashlundt drummed his fingers on his desk some more. He stared up at the ceiling as he waited. I sauntered over and sat next to his chair in support.

Finally, the voice with the formal accent returned to the line. "I'm sorry, Dr. Jaynes, but what is your relationship to Miss Colson?"

Ashlundt ran his hands through his hair. "She's my girlfriend. My fiancé. I'm worried about her welfare. I haven't heard from her since she left for London a month ago."

"I see. Hmm… well policy dictates that I cannot give out this kind of information over the telephone…"

"Look, Mrs. Hyde-White, I'm really worried about her. I just need to make sure she's there and safe at the very least!"

I thought he might throw another book against the wall any second now, but Ashlundt remained surprisingly composed.

"All right. I appreciate your concern. Let me scan the file."

I held my breath waiting for her answer.

"I'm sorry, Dr. Jaynes, but Miss Colson was offered an opportunity here at the department a year ago. Brilliant girl, that. But she declined. The note I have in my file says her circumstances no longer permitted her to leave the States."

I watched Ashlundt's face pale. "You're saying she isn't there?"

"Correct. She is not currently situated at Oxford. I hope this is helpful to you, Dr. Jaynes?"

"Yes… it is, thank you." He ended the call, pounded a fist on his desk and shouted the unthinkable… "She lied to me. Why? And where the hell is she?"

****

Days went by. Ashlundt grew more frantic by the hour. He sat behind his desk dialing other numbers in Sara's address book. When he felt he hit another dead end, he'd lean back in his desk chair, hands on head, staring blankly into space. He didn't eat; he rarely slept. He looked scruffy from not shaving. A few of his remaining patients knocked on his outside office door, yet no amount of barking would move him. He only came to life when I made so much ruckus about being fed that he had to fix me my food. Other than that, no matter what I did, he wouldn't budge. His phone would ring, and he would grab it, only to hang up on the person at the other end if it wasn't Sara or someone who could help him locate her. It was so sad to watch.

He was sitting at his desk staring at the wall again when I decided to try and shake him out of his dark mood. I retrieved a rawhide chew bone from my toy box. Hickory flavor. I began by chewing on it as hard as I could to get Ashlundt's attention. Chomp. Chomp. Crunch. Chomp. The rhythmic crunching must have driven him crazy. Finally, he turned to me and threw his hands in the air. "Luke, you're gonna break a tooth if you don't stop chomping on your bone like that."

That was my cue. I began to growl and slowly brought my left hind foot toward the bone in my mouth. It was as if another dog was trying to steal my treasure. As the foot grew closer, I growled louder and evaded it by turning my head in the other direction. I forced my foot closer to my head again and growled even louder. I pushed my foot back and forth toward my face, then turned and snarled at it. Just as quickly I dropped the bone and flashed my teeth at my "rival" foot, which retreated quickly.

Ashlundt threw back his head with a big belly laugh. "Luke, you… you are… ha ha ha. Too funny! You goofy dog… come here, you silly guy."

I was rewarded for my momentary entertainment with a huge hug that seemed to last longer than usual. He squeezed me to him and continued to laugh. It made me smile inside. I had succeeded in making him smile.

Encouraged by my success, I searched for something, anything in the house to continue to jog him out of his dark mood. I started in the den. It was my favorite room because shutters covered the windows and made it cool in summer. The large L-shaped leather sofa was my favorite place to nap. I had a spot right on the end and could lay with my head resting on the stuffed arm. A nap would have been good about then, but I had work to do. I looked at a picture of the three of us on the fireplace mantle. It was the day Tim and Corky came home from vacation and were introduced to me. I was 10 weeks old. Tim took the happy photo. It jogged back memories of my puppy days. Those first weeks at home were full of excitement. I remembered exploring the huge yard and surrounding woods. Ashlundt had bought three beds for me, one for his home office, another for Sara's office and one for the master bedroom. I looked around the room, but I couldn't find what I needed. I jumped from the sofa and continued my search.

The master bedroom was my next stop. I nosed through the laundry basket. Phew! *Ashlundt better wash his clothes.* It was full of dirty socks and underwear. But never mind that. I needed to find something, anything to help us find Sara. No obvious clues. Sara was such a neat person, and all of her personal items were tucked away or taken with her. Another photo of the two of them wouldn't help. I loved the one on their dresser. It had been taken at a party for patients and their pets at Dr. Wild's house. Ashlundt had thrown Sara in the pool, clothes and all, then jumped in after her. Dr. Wild had snapped the photo of them, heads together and wet, laughing in the water. Unfortunately, that was no help.

Finally, in the kitchen, I saw it. A police magnet on the refrigerator that Sara received after a donation to the LAPD Benevolence Foundation. I pushed it to the edge of the door with my nose until it fell to the floor. Gently, I grabbed it with my teeth and carried it to Ashlundt, dropping it in his lap. He was at his usual spot behind his desk. Startled, he looked down at me. "What is it, boy?"

Ashlundt stared at the magnet, then picked it up and turned it over slowly. "Smart boy, Lukey. I thought about going to the police." He shrugged. "It just makes it so… dire. But you know what? It may be our only chance to find her." He flipped the magnet in the air several times, then stood up.

"Luke, come on. We're going to take a trip down to the police station to report Sara as a missing person."

I cocked my head and looked at him. He was wearing his usual t-shirt and shorts uniform. That just wouldn't do for this occasion. I quickly ran to his bedroom and found Ashlundt's navy blue sports jacket that had been flung over a chair. I grabbed it in my teeth and carried it over to him. I thought it might make him a little more "credible." Besides, with Sara not here to look after him, someone needed to make sure he looked presentable.

"Thanks, boy." Ashlundt flashed me a wide-eyed look. "Sometimes I wonder if you weren't someone's personal assistant in a past life." With that, he pulled on a pair of jeans, loafers and a buttoned-down shirt. The jacket finished off the look I wanted him to have.

****

We sat in some cramped office filled with rolls of yellow police tape and unused road flares. The front desk sergeant had ordered me out of the Chatsworth Station, but Officer Holtzman had chided him. "Oh, for Pete's sake, Harold, let the dog through. He's a handsome one."

I had no idea why Harold thought I'd be a problem. The place had grimy concrete floors and walls and needed a good scrubbing.

"And why do you think she is missing, Dr. Jaynes?" Officer Holtzman asked. He was a short, rotund man who smelled of garlic and cheese. The smell made my stomach growl slightly, and I hoped we could eat soon. I loved cheese.

"Well, we lived together for two years, and suddenly she told me she was going to get her doctorate in England." Ashlundt went on to explain the details of how Sara had disappeared from our lives. "She lied, but that's not like her. Something's happened to her." My master squinted in heavy concern.

"Err, is there the possibility that she wanted to leave you and didn't have the courage to say anything?" Holtzman tipped back in his chair with a knowing look. "These things happen sometimes."

"No, she's not like that. She's straightforward and honest. And if she'd been sick of me she'd have told me!" Ashlundt slapped the table to drive home his point. "No, I'm starting to think that something bad has happened to her. Either that, or she's hiding something from me; doesn't want me to know something's going on with her. But that's just a guess."

I put a paw on his leg and whined at Ashlundt to let him know he was on the right track.

Ashlundt shot me a puzzled look, then went on talking to the detective. "That's her nature. She's very giving, loving. She was extremely upset when she left." He turned back to me and gave me a sideways glance.

"Would anyone have reason to threaten her for any particular reason?" The policeman questioned while scribbling notes on a yellow pad.

"No, absolutely not. She's a kind, thoughtful person. Can't think of anything. I mean, she never mentioned being threatened." I could smell Ashlundt's anguish. He was breathing heavily; sweating profusely.

"Okay, let's calm down. I have to ask these questions. Look, regardless of what you think, doc, she may have had her reasons for leaving. Can you think of anything?"

"No, nothing," my master muttered.

I whined to try and get their attention to no avail.

"Okay." Officer Holtzman tapped his pen on the desk. "Here's what I can do. I'll start entering the info about Ms. Colson into our system. But, I need to get more detail. Then, I can circulate her as a 'missing' on the Police National Computer. Any officer domestically or internationally can contact us if they find out anything helpful."

"Good." Ashlundt leaned forward and wiped his brow with his sleeve. What do you need? Oh, wait, I brought something." Fishing into his sports jacket, he handed Holtzman a piece of paper. "That's her license plate number and the make and model of her car. It's a blue and white Mini Cooper."

"This will help. We'll run it through our database; put a trace on it," Holtzman added the information to the pad in front of him.

"Oh, and you'll need these." Ashlundt handed Holtzman three photos of Sara: One a head shot, a second image of her standing with me in our front yard and another of the two of them together in front of Dodger Stadium. I think the last one was taken by Corky a couple of months ago.

"Okay, this is a good start. Any further description would be helpful. You know, height, weight and so forth," the policeman said as he turned to his computer keyboard.

"Well, she's unusually tall for a woman, as you can see in the photos… a little over six feet, but slender, 130 pounds. She's not a typical Southern California girl – but she was born and raised in L.A. She has long black hair to her waist, dark brown eyes full of mischief, freckles across her nose. She has this heart-shaped face... and a wide smile that shows off perfect-"

"Uh, doc, I get the picture," Holtzman interrupted. "It's clear you care about her. Thanks."

After getting her full name, age and our address and phone number, Holtzman tapped his knuckles on the desk. "Any relatives?"

"Her parents are dead. A car wreck. Sara's an only child."

"Friends?"

"Um... I made this list." He pulled a rumpled page from his pocket and unfolded it. "Dr. Suzi Wild at the Wild Vet Clinic. Girlfriends – Debi, Stephanie and Lauren at school; one of my associates – Dr. Bruce Hines at UCLA, and our neighbors, Tim and Corky Benson – but none of them know where Sara has gone. I've talked to them already. I've looked everywhere." Ashlundt clasped his hands in front of him and rested his elbows on his knees.

"Write 'em all down for me anyway on this form – names, addresses and phone numbers. Anything that'll help us." Holtzman slid a pad of paper across the desk to Ashlundt.

Before Ashlundt could finish writing the last bit of information, Officer Holtzman continued his inquiry. "Any particular places that she frequented?"

"Just work, home and out with me. She did some book signings – she's a published author; wrote a book that grew out of her Masters thesis. It's about unconditional love. She studies psychology. Most of the signings were at conferences – we attended them together," Ashlundt remarked as he scratched his head.

"What about her health? Was it good?"

I started to wag my tail and bark.

"Shhh, Luke! Enough!" Ashlundt commanded me. Then, to the officer he remarked, "Sorry about that. He's still a puppy in many ways. Thanks for letting me bring him inside with us." He sighed in frustration. "Oh, and about Sara's health... she never complained of anything. She's just twenty three. Why'd you ask?"

"Just a thought." The officer leaned forward. "Sometimes even young women have lingering health issues, or mental health issues. You know, like diabetes, high blood pressure, nervous breakdown, that sort of thing."

"No, honestly, I can't think of anything like that." Ashlundt scratched his chin. "I mean, she's had colds, even the flu last year for a few days. But that's really it."

"Okay, well how about your living situation? Did you have any problems before she left?" The policeman asked matter-of-factly.

"Well, uh… I recently was involved in a lawsuit related to my practice. I've been pretty tough on her… I tend to take things out on her a bit…" Ashlundt's face slowly turned red as he spoke the words.

"Take things out? Did it ever get physical?"

"Physical?" Ashlundt stood up from his chair, then quickly sat down. "No, never. I'd never do anything like that. Why'd you ask?"

"Just covering the routine questions; not accusing you of anything." Officer Holtzman scribbled something on his notepad. "Look, doc, we'll do what we can to help you find her. But this hardly sounds like abduction at this point, or anything too serious. From what you tell me, it really sounds like Ms. Colson might've just needed some space for a while. You know women. If you guys were arguing, maybe she just needed some time to cool down. Nothing else you've told me points to anything else."

"So, what should I do next?" Ashlundt implored with outstretched arms. I immediately licked the hand closest to me in support.

"Well, first of all, I suggest you go back to Sara's friends and see if you can't get one of them to open up to you. Maybe someone's protecting her. Also, if you have access, please get us her credit card and ATM info. Maybe a checking account number. We'll run a trace and see if she's been using them, and where."

Ashlundt shrugged his shoulders. "Um, well if she's left any records behind, I'll find them for you. And okay, I'll try her friends again. I just don't know…" He began to choke back his anguish as his voice trailed off.

"Doc, to me it just sounds like a domestic disagreement. If you've been having troubles and taking it out on her…"

"It's not like that!" Ashlundt shot up again from his chair. His reaction startled me, and I let out a loud bark. "Shhh." He flashed me a scolding look.

Officer Holtzman reached over and patted Ashlundt's hand gently. "Listen, most times it's like that, doc. I'll put her in the database like I said. And we'll ask around the neighborhood. In the meantime, talk to your friends again and get me the credit card info. Hopefully, she'll just turn up and make both of our jobs a little easier."

"Is that all you can do?" Ashlundt took the detective's extended hand reluctantly and shook it, knowing the meeting was finished.

"For now. Come back if you don't find her. Unless I have some evidence of foul play, the database and the car and financial traces are the best things we can do."

Officer Holtzman patted me on the head. "Hey boy, how 'bout a donut with sprinkles? Would you like one?" He pointed to a pink box on his desk that I'd been eying since we entered the room. I wagged my tail in the affirmative, and he tossed the pastry in my direction. It never hit the ground; devoured in two quick bites.

****

Somewhere in our house there had to be some evidence to help Ashlundt find Sara's whereabouts. I knew what I had to do when we got home.

Ashlundt shuffled into the kitchen to make us dinner. I followed. He started questioning himself aloud. "Luke, what an idiot I've been! How stupid was I with that policeman?" He filled a pot with water and clanked it onto the stove. Next, he opened a jar of Ragu tomato sauce and dumped it in a smaller pan that he had retrieved from the cabinet. It smelled great. He stirred the sauce with a wooden spoon and broke open a box of spaghetti with the other hand. He waited for the water to boil and mumbled, "Now he thinks I've been abusing her; that she ran away from me! How could he think *that*?"

In frustration, he bent down and opened all the cabinets under the stove. He began to rummage through them, throwing pots and pans across the floor. I couldn't resist getting into the act. I quickly slammed into the cabinet pushing the pots and pans out onto the floor and replacing them with my body. It felt cozy inside the pot cabinet.

"Luke! You're making a mess!" The realization of our ridiculous behavior seemed to dawn on him. He put his hands on his hips and chuckled. "Oh, I see; showing me how stupid I'm being, right?" He bent down to clean up our mess. I howled in amusement.

After dinner, I decided to explore Sara's office. I poked my head inside, stood on my hind legs so I could flip on the wall light switch with my nose, climbed into her chair and surveyed her empty desk top. Nothing there. The house was a mess. Ashlundt hadn't allowed the cleaning ladies to do their job since Sara left. The trash can was overflowing with paper. I easily tipped it over with my big head and scattered the contents on the floor. Dirty tissues. Crumpled papers. An empty tape dispenser. I pawed through them slowly until I came to some pamphlets with hospital buildings on them. Maybe Sara had gone to one of them. I scooped them up in my mouth and took them to Ashlundt. He was just coming from the kitchen. I dropped them at his feet.

"Luke! No! Stop making a mess again!" Ashlundt bent down and gathered the pamphlets in his hands. He started to thumb through one of them, then stood upright and continued to shuffle through the pages until something caught his eye. "What's this? UCLA Medical Center? Is this Sara's?" He shoved the pamphlet under my nose and pointed to a section circled in red.

I jumped up and down on my hind legs to encourage him.

He stared at me thoughtfully and then announced, "I'm gonna try Bruce again, boy." I followed him into his office. Ash snapped on an overhead light and hurried to his desk. I sat down on my bed in the corner. Thankfully for my benefit, Ashlundt hit the speaker phone button, allowing me to hear both ends of the conversation.

"Bruce, I know we've already been over this, but I think I'll go insane if I can't find Sara."

"Ash, you've gotta calm down. I know you're worried about her. It's perfectly normal."

Ashlundt rocked back and forth in his chair, then lurched forward toward the phone. "Listen, since we last spoke I've discovered a few things. I just… I don't know what to do about them."

"What do you mean, Ash? What kind of things? I don't follow."

"Well, for starters, I know that she isn't at Oxford. They have no record of her there. She lied to me! I just can't believe it!" Ashlundt shot up from his desk chair and ran his hands through his long blonde hair.

"I'm sorry, Ash." Hines' voice was filled with compassion. If he knew anything more, he wasn't letting on.

"And that's not all," Ashlundt continued. "I went to the police and filed a report. Now they're out looking for her too." Ashlundt was pacing back and forth now, and I watched him intently.

"The cops? Ash, you can't be serious. Why'd you do that?" Bruce suddenly sounded less confident than usual.

"Oh, c'mon. I had to. If someone abducted her on her way to wherever she was going… how could I live with myself if I didn't do everything to find her?"

"Yeah, fine, I get it." Bruce muttered, sounding agitated. "So, okay, you called the police. Why are you telling me all this?"

Ashlundt sat back down in his chair. He stretched his arms high above his head. "Well, actually, Bruce, when I came home, I found some pamphlets in Sara's office. UCLA Medical Center. They had your department circled in red. The handwriting is hers." Ashlundt paused, picked up a pen and rolled it through his fingers nervously. "So, if you know something, it's time you share it! No doubt, the police are probably going to be asking all our friends anyway. I figured I'd give you a heads up."

"Ash, I told you: I don't know where Sara is. Why don't you believe me?" His voice was on shaky grounds now.

"Because you've never been a good liar, Bruce. I'm sick with worry and need to know if she's okay." Ashlundt leaned forward in his chair, placing his elbows on his knees. "What are you hiding from me?"

"Look, Ash, stop worrying about her; I'm sure she'll contact you when she can."

"Okay, now you *can't* tell me you don't know something!" Ashlundt leaped to his feet in anger again shaking his fist in the air.

"Really, I don't know anything, Ash!"

"Bruce, you're lying." He bent toward the speaker phone, hands on hips, as if to accuse it.

"Ash, I'm not lying. Stop bullying me about this."

"Bullying? Bruce, how would you feel if our situations were reversed?"

"I… I don't know what you mean."

"Bruce, you've always been a good friend. Please help me; I beg you. Plus, now the cops are involved. If you have a lead…" Ashlundt sighed, not completing his sentence.

"I can't do anything to help you, Ash. Wish I could."

"Listen, meet me at Starbucks on Weyburn in Westwood. It's close to you. I need a friend. C'mon, man. Please?" Ashlundt seemed to be begging the speaker phone now, both hands clasped together. I got up from my bed and moved closer to him. His hand immediately found my head and scratched it nervously.

"Well, I'm in the middle of a project right now. It's a bad time."

Ashlundt leaned toward the speaker. "Please, Bruce."

Dr. Hines hesitated for a moment. I could hear papers being shuffled.

"The best I can do is later, after work, Ash. I'll be done here by nine, maybe later."

"Fine, I'll be there at nine, Bruce. I'll wait for you 'til you get there."

Ashlundt paced around the house until it was time to leave. We loaded into his SUV, and I settled behind him and took a nap. I hoped Dr. Hines would provide us with the answers we needed.

****

It was a warm, comfortable evening. We sat at an outdoor table. Ashlundt sipped his iced coffee and rubbed my neck beneath my collar as we waited. I could feel his palms getting sweaty as his watch ticked onward. The coffee shop was pretty crowded for nighttime. A number of couples were sitting outside at tables throughout the patio with sweet smelling beverages. Ashlundt also mumbled something about some of them being students in study groups, whatever that was.

"Quarter to ten!" Ashlundt blurted out at one point. It was a few moments later when Dr. Hines finally appeared. He walked slowly to our table and shook hands with Ashlundt, then gave me a solid body rub that got my leg to shake involuntarily. It felt so good. Dr. Hines headed inside and ordered some coffee. Soon, he was back at our table. He seemed nervous. He was a thin man with dark brown hair and eyes somewhat obscured by dark horned-rim glasses.

"So, Ash, how's the lawsuit going?" His coffee cup revealed the slightest tremble while he held it to add extra sugar from a paper packet.

"I settled it, Bruce. Attorney cleaned me out. Insurance covered the settlement."

I could tell that Ashlundt was holding himself back. He kept bouncing his left leg off the ball of his foot in a nervous tick.

"Business hasn't been so good."

"Sorry to hear it. Such a bum deal."

"Yeah. It was bad enough having my patient die like that… I thought I had her in a better place… it was horrible." Ashlundt sipped his iced coffee again and continued to bounce his left leg while rubbing my head even harder as I sat closely next to him.

There was an awkward pause between the two of them with both men fidgeting. And then, Ashlundt took the plunge.

"Bruce, I can't avoid the reason I'm here any longer. Please, if you know anything about Sara, you gotta tell me."

"I told you, Ash, I know nothing." Dr. Hines wiped his face with a napkin.

I knew it was a lie. He was sweating. I could smell it. He also refused to look Ashlundt in the eyes when he told it. If there's one thing dogs know about sincerity, it's eye contact.

"Bruce, why are you doing this? I know damn well you're lying. You can't even look me in the face." Ashlundt leaned forward in his chair toward his friend. He'd picked up on the same concern that I'd noticed.

"That's not true!" Dr. Hines hunched forward and looked somewhere between Ashlundt's nose and mouth.

"Look, how long have we been friends? Fifteen years?"

"Oh, I don't know. Since we were teenagers, right? High school, I guess," Dr. Hines admitted as he played with the stir stick in his coffee cup.

"Then why are you refusing to share what you know with me? I'm... I'm just sick with worry about Sara. I've been to the police. I've called everyone I know. If you truly don't know where she is, then I'll be terrified that something awful has happened to her." Ashlundt sat back in his chair, sighed deeply and ran his hands through his hair.

"I don't know what you want me to say, Ash." Dr. Hines shrugged.

I need you to look me in the eyes and tell me you don't know where she is, Bruce."

Hines looked at Ashlundt and once again repeated, "I don't know..."

"Bruce, let me level with you. Tomorrow morning I have to go back to the police with her credit card and ATM info. If she's alive and using her money, they're going to be able track her down through recent transactions. And it's not just that. Bruce, the cops are starting to point a finger at me. I'm the last one who supposedly saw her alive. If she stays missing any longer, well, I could be arrested. I think the investigating officer thinks that I was abusive with her. So now, it's not just about her. It's about me too. If you know anything at all, now would be the ideal time to share it. For everyone's sake."

Dr. Hines rubbed the back of his thin neck and let out a deep sigh. "Look, I promised Sara. She's... trying to protect you. But, we've been friends for a long time."

"Protect me? From what? Bruce, damn it! Tell me what you know!" Ashlundt glared at his friend.

"Sara has... Sara's been ill. I-"

I barked twice out loud to confirm that Bruce was telling the truth. Ashlundt ignored me, his eyes fixed on those of his friend.

"What? Sick! What's happened to her?" Ashlundt leaped from his chair. "Please, Bruce, please tell me about Sara!"

The conversations from the surrounding tables seemed to stop at once. Everyone on the coffee shop patio was staring at us.

Dr. Hine leaned closer to Ashlundt and spoke in a hushed tone. "In the five weeks since she left you, Sara had a mastectomy... cancer... She's just starting chemo."

"Oh, my God!" Ashlundt fell back into his chair. The color drained from his face. Several moments passed. He just sat quietly with his head in his hands. I inched closer to him and licked his cheek in an effort to console him. I think I tasted a few teardrops.

Finally, Ashlundt looked up at Dr. Hines. He whispered, "Where is she?"

"Ash, please just wait until Sara contacts you. She will, you know." Again, Hines wiped the sweat from his brow with a napkin.

"I need to know where she *is*, Bruce!" Ashlundt slammed his fist on the glass table again drawing the attention of onlookers around us.

"I'm not going to tell you that, Ash."

"Why?"

Dr. Hines took another sip of his coffee. He wiped his forehead with his hands. "She already had the diagnosis and scheduled the surgery when she left you."

"My God, she told me nothing," Ashlundt replied, anguish in his voice.

"It had been her plan to call you the first week she left to keep up the pretense, but she had a rough time with the surgery. Then, after you started calling all her friends, well, she knew you were on to her."

"So, her friends are in on this?" Ashlundt stared at the star-filled sky and said nothing.

Hines reached across the table and placed his hand on his friend's arm. "I'll need to tell her that I talked to you. I'm sorry, Ash."

Ashlundt said nothing. He sat for what seemed a long time until I finally put my head in his lap and gave him a sympathetic whine. "Why?" he moaned. "Why did this have to happen?"

I whined again, put my paws in his lap and pushed the top of my body into it, licking his face and trying to console him. Gently, he pushed me back down.

Ashlundt straightened himself in his chair and looked up at his friend. "You won't tell me where she is? Is she at UCLA?"

Dr. Hines averted his eyes and stared at his coffee cup. "I'm so sorry, Ash. I won't say anymore. I've already violated her trust enough."

Ashlundt stood and placed his empty cup in the nearby trash. "Well, thanks for being honest, Bruce. I gotta go now. Gotta figure out what to tell the police tomorrow."

He took my leash and pulled me away. I turned back to the table. I could tell that Dr. Hines was probably equally as upset as we were.

Ashlundt was unusually silent on the way home. I expected he would make frantic calls to all of Sara's friends, especially Debi… or try to find her at UCLA now.

But, something I hadn't expected happened. Ashlundt changed into a pair of sweat pants, crawled into bed and wrestled with his blankets for hours until finally falling asleep. My instincts told me that his search for Sara had ended tonight. That his attempt to track her down concluded with the revelation of her hidden illness. He was no longer filled with worry about her disappearance. Now, he was angry and pained that she had left him without telling the truth.

Luke's Tale

Chapter Four

The Healing

My worst fears were realized the next morning.

Ashlundt woke up and stumbled into the shower. I headed out back and took the opportunity to thoroughly water all the plants in the yard. To top that exercise off, I managed a big drink from my automatic outside water feeder. It left me a little wet around the collar, but nothing I couldn't easily shake off. When I sauntered into the kitchen, I found Ashlundt standing over the stove scrambling eggs. The room smelled like burnt toast, with some coffee brewing on the side. Luckily for me, he scraped a few bits of egg from the pan into my kibble before sitting it on the floor for me.

Ashlundt gobbled down his breakfast, leaving his pan and dishes in the sink. We headed out for a short walk around the block. But, when we got back, instead of returning to his Sara-hunting activities, his nervous energies took him in a completely different direction. "Luke, my boy, gotta get to work; start rebuilding my business," he declared as he hung up my leash.

He began by typing letters to all his clients to explain to them his situation with the lawsuit. He wanted them to know that he wasn't guilty of wrong-doing. Sometimes he'd read them out loud, as if to be certain that he worded them correctly. As if I could help him to edit them... but still, I appreciated knowing what he was up to.

Standing and stretching after he finished the last letter, he turned away from his desk when the phone rang. He punched the speaker phone button. "Ashlundt Jaynes."

"Oh, hi, doc. It's Holtzman at the Chatsworth PD."

Ashlundt plopped back down in his chair.

"Hi, I was gonna call you. Listen…"

"Sorry, doc, just wanted you to know that Miss Colson's car was spotted in Brentwood yesterday. The reporting officer said that the driver of the vehicle somewhat matched the photos we have of her."

Ashlundt paused for a second. "Really? Yes. I… uh… I learned last night that she isn't really missing."

"It's what I thought then." Holtzman's voice cracked over the speaker. "She needed some time away, right?"

Ashlundt sat back in his chair and pushed his hair away from his face. "Guess you had it pegged."

"Yeah, I have an instinct about these things." I could hear the policeman's ego all the way through the speaker phone. "Am I right in thinking you'll want to remove the missing person's report on her?"

Ashlundt chewed his lip and appeared not to know what to say next. "Uh, yeah. I'm sorry to have troubled you, officer."

"No trouble. Glad she's okay. And, doc, you might be smart not to take your troubles out on your lady friend next time." Holtzman's end of the line clicked off.

Ashlundt sat there for a few moments almost in shock. Suddenly he wiped his face with his hand and bolted to the bathroom.

A quick salad for lunch in the kitchen, with a few slices of ham for me, and Ashlundt was back at his desk. It was as if he had merely taken a routine lunch break. I was baffled by his behavior.

Ashlundt made dozens of calls to other patients, offering them some free sessions if they'd come back and work with him. He was driven. Looking at me after a long day of calls in his office, he declared, "Got to stabilize the finances, boy. Didn't have the energy to do it after that terrible tragedy with my patient."

I put my paw on his knee and cocked my head to try and show that I understood. He pulled out a piece of paper from his desk and stared at it for a moment. "Twenty-five thousand in attorney fees! And for what? So insurance could pay a quarter of a mil in settlement fees. I should have fought it. My malpractice rates are gonna be off the charts. But, what can you do?"

I was thankful that he always talked to me as if I was his best friend. The more I discovered, the easier it was for me to try and help him. Like the time he wanted to surprise Sara with her new car for her birthday. We sat in his office, and he gave me specific instructions. "Take her for a long walk in the woods, Luke. You know, sniff every leaf; pee on every tree. Go way past the equestrian center. Make her chase you for a while. I need time to get the Mini Cooper out of Tim's garage and into mine. And everybody needs time to get here and hide."

I barked twice in compliance, then took off to nag Sara until she took me out. With ball and leash in my mouth, I sauntered into her office and pushed her hand off her computer keyboard.

"Luke! I'm in the middle of work."

I flashed her my most adorable look and sat up on my hind legs with a ball and leash still in tow. She melted. Ashlundt and I pulled off a successful surprise.

The months on the calendar rolled by slowly. The seasons changed, and Sara still hadn't returned. Ashlundt continued calling his former clients to regain their confidence. He did nothing to try and track down Sara, though, at times I sensed he was lost in thought about her. I would lie on my bed in his office and watch as he stared at the wall or ceiling, often blinking back a small tear that gathered in the corner of his eye. Occasionally he'd wander into her office, running his hand over the top of her desk or the back of her chair. Once, I followed him into the bedroom and watched as he pulled down one of her old sweatshirts and brought it into his bed. Sort of like how I always pulled my Teddy Bear into my bed and used it as a pillow each night.

To shake him out of it, I went into an immediate routine of chasing my own tail. I swirled round and round, barking and continuing the merry chase but to no avail. Nothing seemed to bring him back from his loneliness.

After what seemed like hundreds (I wasn't *that* good at math) of evening meals, I decided to bring him reminders of her. If Ashlundt had buried his pain, well, I sure hadn't. I needed to find a way to bring them back together.

I started with keepsakes that Sara had left behind. She often smelled like fresh cut flowers, and I could scent her on anything she had touched or worn. I hoped she hadn't taken her silver charm bracelet Ashlundt had given her. The one that matched my collar. I plodded into the master bedroom and jumped onto the chair next to the dresser. I recalled that she usually kept the bracelet in her jewelry box. To open it, I had to pull the metal handle with the toenails on my right front paw. Thankfully the box didn't have a lock or clasp. There it was, sitting right on top. I was surprised she hadn't taken it with her; I guessed she had forgotten it. Carefully, I clasped it with my teeth and lowered it on to the top of the dresser, before letting go. I did my best to quietly close the box drawer with my nose. Next, I grabbed the bracelet again in my teeth and jumped down off the chair. The bed was just three steps away. I took a running leap, headed for Ashlundt's pillow and gently dropped the bracelet in the middle.

Next, I grabbed my fancy silver collar from my toy box next to my bed in the master bedroom. I didn't wear this one unless we were going out because it jingled. I also had a plain one for occasions when I didn't want to dress up. I would always bring one of them to Ashlundt, or Sara when we were going away from home. I could always find them with my toys.

Finally, I noticed a recent photo of the two of them that Sara had framed, but not had time to hang. She was sitting on Ashlundt's lap on the patio steps in Tim and Corky's backyard. He was tickling her, and she was laughing. Corky had captured a great candid shot of them. It was on a table next to the closet. I knew I needed to hide these treasures until the appropriate time.

I snuck out through the doggie door in the kitchen with all these items dangling from my mouth. It was no easy trick. No matter how hard I tried, the items banged against the frame of my door. I ended up dropping the bracelet twice. Finally, I decided to take each item through the door, one-at-a-time. I found what I thought to be the right spot. Carefully, I brought each item to the ground next to it and began to dig a deep hole. I frantically dug for about five minutes. I was covered in dirt. Finally, I stopped to inspect my work. The hole was plenty large enough for everything, so I gently placed my treasures in it. I then reversed my digging angle and covered them with the excavated dirt. I wanted them to have dirt on them so that when I dropped them on him, he'd have to deal with cleaning them too. Well, it made perfect sense to me!

I finished the deed by marking the spot. A good roll in the grass and a solid shake rid me of all evidence of my covert activities.

****

Ashlundt was on the phone again the next morning. We sat in his office while he finished a series of calls. His inaction to find Sara left me frustrated. I hurried to the backyard to uncover one of my treasures. Pouncing on what I thought was the right spot, I dug only to discover a long-forgotten bone. Setting it aside for a good chew later, I sniffed the yard until I found the spot. Again digging methodically, I hit pay dirt. The silver charm bracelet was first to surface. I scooped it up, then recovered the hole. I could barely contain myself as I ran in and dropped it in his lap.

"Luke! What's this? It's filthy." Upon closer inspection his eyes widened. "Sara's bracelet? What the… Where'd you get this?" His raised eyebrows made it clear that he was totally confused.

I barked loudly and dogged him as he carried it into the kitchen and washed it carefully in the sink, then wiped it clean with a dish towel. He turned to me and spoke in a scolding voice as he pointed to the bracelet. "No, Luke! Don't bother Sara's things."

I stood and wagged my tail. That angered him even more.

"No, Luke! Get out! In the backyard, bad dog!" He slapped my behind hard. Ouch! My butt throbbed. I winced and gave out a loud yelp. I scurried out of the kitchen, my nails scraping on the brick floor. Out through my doggie door, I dashed into the backyard and flopped down and rolled on a spot that smelled like raccoon droppings. *Ashlundt was so dense! What was wrong with him? How could he do nothing about Sara?*

The next morning, as he sat in the den reading the newspaper, I crept out my doggie door and searched the yard for my hiding place. In my haste, I hadn't covered the hole properly and quickly latched onto my matching silver collar. I took my time to carefully cover the remaining photograph. My cautious mood continued as I slowly entered the den and dumped it next to him. He was so surprised that he stared at it with his mouth hanging wide open. He flashed me an angry look, jumped up and grabbed me by the back of my neck. "Bad dog, Luke! No! You've got dirt all over me! The sofa's a mess!" He turned on his heels and headed straight for the kitchen. Again, I followed him and watched as he cleaned the collar, then stomped off into his bedroom, dropping it in my toy box. I cautiously entered the room, afraid of another spanking. He turned to me and glared with disgust, then stomped out of the room, slamming the door behind him. I was locked in until dinner time. There was nothing to do but mope and wonder what it was going to take to motivate him to get in touch with Sara.

On day three of my campaign, after my evening meal, Ashlundt looked at me with raised eyebrows, still annoyed. "I've got a community event, Luke. I should leave you home as punishment. Bad dog! But you always charm the pants off potential clients. Go get your collar, unless you buried it again!"

His wish was my command. I grabbed it from the toy box, along with my Teddy Bear for the ride.

Ashlundt had participated in several community events to gain positive exposure over the prior few weeks. They were held at church recreational centers or various meeting rooms in Chatsworth or Woodland Hills. This one was being hosted by a real estate office for people new to the area. Ashlundt was a participating sponsor and got to give a brief presentation. He offered an initial free counseling session at the end of his talk as an incentive to get people to try him. Several took advantage.

I reeled in the first one. She was a real dog lover who introduced herself as Kate Brown. Ashlundt began to show her how I could hi-five.

"Dr. Jaynes, while I have you here. My 15-year-old son's having problems adjusting to our move. We've lived in the same place since he was born, and now he's lonely and misses his friends." She knelt down next to me and scratched my ears, and I melted against her so she wouldn't stop. Unfortunately, she stood up straight and looked Ashlundt in the eye. "Do you think a few sessions with you might help him?"

"Very likely, Mrs. Brown. I've had a number of teenaged patients struggling with change." He casually reached into his jacket pocket and pulled out a business card. "Sometimes having someone that's not close to them to share their feelings helps them gain perspective. Here's my card; please call me, and we'll set up an appointment."

"Thanks; I'll call tomorrow." She gave me one last head rub and moved off into the crowd.

"I knew you'd be a charmer and come in handy, Luke," Ashlundt said under his breath. "Good boy."

A Southern accent floated toward us. "Oh, Dr. Jaynes, I'm so delighted that awful mess is behind you." It was Peggy Cummings, the realtor who was hosting the event. "You and Luke are certainly a big hit tonight. Wouldn't be surprised that you get a bunch of patients out of this."

"Thanks for letting me participate, Peggy." Ashlundt nodded his appreciation.

"As a matter of fact, I was wondering. Do you do marriage counseling?"

While they chatted, I wandered off to check out the refreshment table. I was sure if I hung around long enough someone would sucker up and feed me some of the leftover crackers, or maybe a slab of roast beef. Nothing like food to take your mind off your troubles.

****

"Nobody understands how much I miss my friends. My parents only think about *themselves.*" The boy anguished over his recent move to California.

"Kevin, it was your mother's concern for you that brought you here to me," Ashlundt responded in his calm but assertive psychologist's manner. Ashlundt was in the middle of one of those free sessions in the late afternoon in his home office with Kate Brown's son. It was the perfect time to give Ashlundt another reminder. I didn't think Kevin's problems were serious enough that they couldn't be interrupted. Actually, Ashlundt looked like he could use a break. I got up from my bed next to his consultation chair directly across from the patient sofa and stretched my paws. Casually, I walked out of the office, down the hall to the kitchen, and through the doggie door to the backyard. I started to get excited about jogging Ashlundt's memory. Frantically, I dug up the framed picture of Ashlundt and Sara and ran back to the office. The glass was covered in mud. It left droppings across his office as I skidded in, then gently laid it in his lap. The filthy frame smeared dirt down Ashlundt's pant leg. He stared at it and shook his head. I barked my approval. Ashlundt gritted his teeth and glared at me.

"Luke! Bad dog! Go lie down!" Then, he looked at his patient. "I'm so sorry, Kevin. I'm having some discipline problems with my dog. Excuse me while I clean this up."

"It's okay, doc. I need to pee anyway." Kevin smirked as if amused and headed toward the office bathroom. He shut the door behind him.

I followed Ashlundt into the hall. He was trying so hard to keep his professional composure with his client still within an earshot. When he heard my collar jingling, he turned around and whispered, "Luke, will you stop with this! I get the message. I'm just not ready yet!"

Ah, so he *was* starting to get it. You could've fooled me. Except for getting angry with me, he'd been absolutely emotionless about my other *reminders.* What was wrong with him? I didn't understand until now. But at least for a moment, I had a glimmer of hope to cling to.

****

It was seven evening meals later. I sat in his consultation area next to his office, when I recognized a familiar face peeking in and knocking at Ashlundt's patient entrance. It was pudgy Mrs. Ford with the brightly dyed red hair. Ashlundt referred to her as bi-polar, and she was always either bouncing off the walls with exuberance, or in a deep depression. That day, she came bouncing in. "Lukey, my boy! How are you? You cute, fuzzy little boy. Come here and let Auntie Amelia give you a hug." She squeezed me so tightly that I thought she'd broken my ribs.

I followed her into the office. Ashlundt greeted her warmly. "Mrs. Ford, I'm delighted that you've decided to come back."

Things were starting to pick up. Over the course of the next 30 evening meals, several more of Ashlundt's old clients started to return. I recognized quite a few of them by their faces, and others by their smell. Mrs. Hassenfield, the addictive personality, always wore fancy open-toed shoes. Mr. Robbins, the anger management construction worker, usually smelled like cigarettes and coffee. A few new faces were also showing up. One woman called Michelle was so impressed with my ability to perform tricks that she began to bring me bribery treats for each of her next several visits. Sit ups, high-fives, roll overs – you name it; I could do them for a couple of breadsticks, or animal crackers. *I was such a clever boy when I was hungry, which was almost always.*

I was terribly proud of Ashlundt for the way he managed to gradually revive his practice. I had been so worried about him in the weeks after Sara had left. He had been a terrible mess. But with the passage of time, he had begun shaving again, dressing in professional clothing when he had patients over, and actually seeing clients in his office. It was a welcome change for us both. That was the good news.

On the flip side, there seemed to be no movement on his part to try and locate Sara. In counting my filled dinner bowls, I was able to make it to 120 since Ashlundt and Dr. Hines had met at Starbucks. What Ashlundt called Christmas had come and gone quietly. His family tried to get us to come to San Diego for the holidays, but he refused saying he had to work. I couldn't even begin to count how long it had been since Sara had left us. I know she left us in warm weather in the summertime. Then, the cool weather passed us by, and it was warm again. The flowers were in full bloom. It had been way too long. I missed her and decided to start reapplying the reminders.

One thing about Ashlundt: he hated it when things were moved away from places where he'd left them. He'd get crazy when he couldn't find his socks, his wristwatch or his pens. So you can only imagine his reaction when I went back into the bedroom, grabbed Sara's charm bracelet and the once-buried framed photo and dragged them back to his office… just after one of his newest clients had completed a session.

The photograph of them laughing together was the last straw. He was reading his notes when I laid it on his lap. He exploded. "What are you doing to me?" Ashlundt reached for a big Yellow Pages phonebook, picked it up and hoisted it onto the floor. Thwack! It landed about a German Shepherd's length from where I was standing. Now, I was mad. I began barking at the top of my lungs. This was behavior I rarely exhibited, but surely necessary in that moment of desperation.

Ashlundt grew angrier. He stamped his foot in my general direction and began to shout. "Luke. Knock it off! Now! I'm warning you, no supper tonight if you don't calm the hell down!"

I wouldn't calm down. If one bowl of K-Dog was my sacrifice for getting Sara back, I was willing to starve for at least one night. Only my barking seemed to have the opposite effect on Ashlundt. Instead of motivating him to action, he seemed to just get madder at me.

The more I barked, the more things he threw on the floor. A paper weight. His appointment book. A computer speaker. Finally, I was starting to feel threatened. I leaped onto his chest, catching him off balance in his anger, and brought him to the floor. We hit the carpet together alongside his desk with a muffled thud.

My master flashed me a puzzled look. He was still breathing heavily; his heart was pounding like a jackhammer. So was mine. It took both of us a moment to gather our senses. And then something amazing happened. Ashlundt's anger subsided into sighs of frustration, then tears. He began to wail; a sadness I had never witnessed before in my life. Tears were flowing steadily down his cheeks. I did what any loyal canine would do. I licked his face and hands as he curled with his arms around his legs on the floor. Then, I sat directly in front of him and waited.

Eventually, Ashlundt sat up. He wiped his eyes with the bottom of his shirt. And then he looked at me. I nudged the picture of the two of them with my nose until it rested next to his feet.

"I know, Luke, I know. I'm such a bastard. But I can't stand to see her suffering and sick!" He ran his fingers through his long shaggy hair, then stared at the ground.

I was flabbergasted. *How did this once charming man become such a coward? I recalled how gentle and understanding he was with one young housewife who was trying to cope with her own cancer. She had been deeply depressed, and he helped her realize how much her family loved her. "You need to not give up; fight the cancer for the sake of those who love you so much," he had told her. How could he take such good care of his patients and not be there for his greatest love? Perhaps it had something to do with what he had mentioned to Tim. Something about being so emotionally involved with Sara but detached from his patients? Well, anyway, it sounded good.*

I barked once and pushed the photo up against his leg with my nose. He said nothing; just stared at it in silence. I couldn't tell you precisely how long it was that we just sat there, but I know it was until long after the sun went down. Eventually, I pushed the photo frame between his legs, put my paw on his knee, then looked at the phone. He followed my gaze and let out a deep sigh. "Okay. You win. I know what I need to do, boy. Enough."

Ashlundt staggered up from the floor and fell with a thump into his chair. He rifled through his papers on the desk until he found what he was looking for. Then, he reached for the phone. First, he pressed the speaker phone button. A loud dial tone filled the room. Next, he punched in eleven digits on the keypad. There was a ringing for a moment, then an answer.

"Good evening. Dr. Hines' office."

"Um, yes… hi. May I speak with Dr. Hines please? Tell him it's Dr. Jaynes."

I walked back to my doggie bed and sat waiting for their conversation to play out.

Soon, a familiar voice was on the line, this one a man. "Ash. How are you?"

"Bruce, I'm… I've been better. But more importantly, how's Sara? Is she there?"

There was a long pause. I could almost hear Dr. Hines struggling with the answer. "Yes… yes, my friend, she's here," Hines replied. "But not too loud, okay? She swore us all to secrecy."

"All of you? You mean the doctors, the staff, her girlfriends? Does everyone but me know?" Ashlundt shrugged his anguish.

"Of course, Ash. She needed people to help her get through this."

"You don't need to lay on the guilt, Bruce. But her friends all work. How did that play out?"

Dr. Hines hesitated. "I'm not going into detail. I can't now. Let's just say her friends got her through the roughest parts, Ash."

"Is Sara better?" Ashlundt's voice shook with the question.

"After a lengthy stay here at the Center… Look, Ash, I can't tell you anymore. Confidentiality, you know."

Ashlundt leaned forward toward the speaker phone and rubbed the back of his neck. "Bruce, I know I've been a real heel about all this. Please, just give me an update."

"Why, Ash? So you can feel better? Do you have any clue how much you hurt her when you ignored her after you knew the truth?"

Ashlundt stood up. "What? How did she know? Did you tell her?"

"Of course I told her, Ash! I thought you'd try to make contact with her. You can be such an ass." Dr. Hines hissed the last word.

"Please, Bruce. Firstly, you told me not to bother her when we last spoke. We... I think we need to have another face-to-face. I have so many questions. And, I promise you I won't let Sara down this time."

I got up from my bed and walked next to Ashlundt to show my encouragement. My tail was wagging like windshield wipers in a hurricane.

"Man, how could you have just ignored her for the past year? My faith in you is at an all-time low." Dr. Hines' voice was filled with accusation.

Ashlundt took a deep breath. "I know, but you... Look, just meet me, please? Okay?"

"Can I really believe you, man? You know, you don't deserve her at all."

"I know I don't. Look, I love her. I screwed this one up. I need to make it right. Please meet me, Bruce?"

Dr. Hines was silent. Ashlundt looked as if he would explode, and then he did. "Look, Bruce, *you* were the one who wouldn't tell me where she was. *You told me not to contact her. You* said she wanted to keep this from me. Why are you forgetting all of that!"

"Hold on, Ash. I was just trying to protect Sara. I thought you'd walk through walls to find her!" Dr. Hines' anguish was palpable. He let out a deep breath and stayed silent for what seemed like an eternity. Only his breathing could be heard through the speaker.

Finally, Ashlundt spoke up. "Bruce, you still there? Are we meeting up, or what?"

"Yeah, fine. I suppose I could for a few minutes. Same Starbucks. Same time. And you're buying my coffee this time."

I was so excited that I could hardly wait to get my collar from the toy box. Snatching it quickly, I skidded into his office and sat up begging to go. "Of course, you'll go, Luke. It's a couple hours away, though. Let's get some chow."

*****

We were early. Ashlundt waited to get his coffee until Dr. Hines arrived. The cooler weather had most of the other patrons huddled inside. Ashlundt elected to sit close to a space heater on the patio. He fiddled with his keys as he sat nervously and gazed at the full moon behind the tall hospital buildings.

At last, Dr. Hines arrived. He looked drawn and tired as he rushed over to our table in his green hospital scrubs.

"Sorry I'm late, Ash. Busy day." They shook hands and went inside for coffee. I waited on the patio, watching the cars come and go from the small parking lot next door. When they returned, Dr. Hines was still sounding less than his friendly self.

Ashlundt settled down at a table and pounced with a barrage of questions. "So, how's she doing? What's her prognosis? Did you treat her? Did you use an experimental procedure? Where's she living now?"

Hines held up his hands, palms first, at his friend. "Whoa, slow down, Ash. First, I need something from you."

Ashlundt was rocking back and forth on his chair. "Sure. Anything. You just tell me."

"Ash, I need your word that you won't hurt Sara again. You have to at least seek her out on your own. I wouldn't tell you anything, but if there's a glimmer of hope you can make her happy…"

Ashlundt reached out a hand and placed it on his friend's arm. "I swear, Bruce. Please tell me."

Hines stared at the hand on his arm. "Okay, prognosis is good. She's been through some intense rounds of chemo. And no, I didn't treat her. I couldn't tell you anything if I did."

"Is the cancer gone?" Ashlundt fidgeted with his hands, almost ringing them with anticipation.

"Looks good enough for her to get reconstructive surgery." I pressed close to Ashlundt with the good news.

"Thank, God," Ashlundt breathed a long sigh of relief and sat back in his chair. "Is the surgery soon?"

"Not sure. She had intended to call you once it was over, but now, I dunno." Dr. Hines looked down and shook his head, stirred his coffee, then took a sip of it.

"Is she working? How is she surviving?" Ashlundt leaned toward his friend.

"She went through the counseling program here, and now she's counseling other cancer patients.

"How could she have handled all the bills? I know she has insurance, but it must've been rough."

Dr. Hines took another sip of his coffee and shifted uncomfortably in his chair. "She tapped into the money her parents left her – the trust."

Ashlundt wrung his hands and whispered, "Oh, God."

I moved closer to Dr. Hines and put my paw on his knee. It was my way of saying thanks for the information. He stroked my head, and I gave him a large open-mouthed smile.

"What hours is she working in the clinic, Bruce?"

"She'll be in tomorrow morning at 8:00, most likely 'til about 5 or 6, but why don't you let me talk to her first?" Dr. Hines took a long sip of his cinnamon-smelling coffee.

Again Ashlundt placed his hand on his friend's arm as if to caution him. "No! No go-betweens, Bruce. Don't say anything to her. Let me talk to her. I have a lot of explaining to do. It'll be better received face-to-face with me. It'll seem insincere if you plead my case."

Dr. Hines sighed deeply. "All right, Ash, but know that Sara didn't run away to hurt you. She's been through hell and back. She didn't want you to have to suffer through it if things didn't turn out as well as they have. When you didn't try to see her after the last time we spoke…" his voice trailed off, and I again put my paw on his knee.

Ashlundt fiddled with his empty coffee cup. "Why did you tell her, Bruce? I don't understand."

"When you didn't contact her, I tried to get her to call you. But now she thinks you don't care. So, don't be hard on her."

"Hard on her? Do you think I'm a monster? It's me that needs a kick in the butt. I need to beg her forgiveness."

I shifted uncomfortably back to Ashundt's side. I thought that begging would not be enough. Knowing how much Sara loved

Ashlundt and how hurt she would be, I could only imagine that he was going to have to do some major groveling. But I'd already provided enough helpful hints to get us to this point. A minor victory in the bigger picture.

Luke's Tale

Chapter Five

The Forgiving

He put me on a stay next to the door and went to sit in the lobby very early the next morning. She saw me before she could enter the front entrance at the medical center a short time later.

"Luke! My God, it's you!" She ran and knelt down to me, her thin arms embracing my wagging body as I covered her face with kisses. I could no longer smell the cancer. This was a really good sign!

"How are you here, boy?" she asked. "Is he here with you?" I barked my response and looked over at Ashlundt through the glass. She followed my gaze.

He stood as she walked into the building and pulled her lightweight leather jacket around her chest as if to hide from him. She was wiping perspiration from her face. Her even thinner body began to shake. She appeared to have lost a considerable amount of weight. But to me, she was still beautiful.

Before she could do or say anything, Ashlundt ran to her and embraced her so hard that it had to have taken away her breath. I winced as I watched. Slowly, he dropped to his knees while still holding her in his arms. I managed to slip in through the electric doors behind a nurse. Rather than disturb their moment, I chose to sit in a corner close enough to hear them.

Looking up at her, he asked, "Sara, I... I'm so... sorry."

Her body was rigid; she said nothing.

He buried his head in her skirt and begged, "Forgive me, Sara. I was so blinded by wallowing in my own self-pity that I couldn't see what you were going through. At first, I had no idea. I never knew that you were sick. But I'm not mad at you for not telling me."

Sara nodded slightly in recognition. Ashlundt took a deep breath, then continued his apology. "Please know that I love you no matter what. You never have to go away from me again." He looked at her face and whispered, "Please forgive me."

Her body remained rigid and unyielding. "Forgive you? I would if it was only that you couldn't see what I was going through before I left. But once you *knew – you knew*, and you didn't try to reach out to me!"

"No listen, Sara, I… Bruce said you didn't want me to know… and… I just wasn't ready to… to see you… ill," he pleaded.

"I… I… I, Ash. It's always about you, isn't it? Well, this time, what the hell about me? I didn't know what to do. It was really bad. I… I lost my left breast. I've gone through chemo." She ran one hand through her now very short dark hair. "I knew that if I put this on you it would hold you back from what you needed to do. I didn't want you to have to go through what you did with your brother. You couldn't take another blow. I *was* thinking only of you and what you needed. But, when you pried the truth out of Bruce, what did you do for me? Did you love me enough to even see how I was doing?"

"But, Bruce said it was going well for you, Sara. He told me you didn't want me to know anything. It was so hard, but I wanted to respect your wishes. I never thought that you wouldn't be all right. He said you were going to be all right. I-"

"But, you knew! You knew!" Sara shouted as her face turned fire engine red. Then remembering her surroundings, she whispered, "If our roles had been reversed, do you think *anything* could have kept me from being at your side?" she whispered.

The look of guilt spread across his face like a disease that I could smell from my corner.

"But you left me, Sara. You hid your illness from me. You didn't want me to know. I thought you were at Oxford for a while, only I couldn't reach you. I went to the police; filed a report. I finally got Bruce to tell me the truth. And he told me you didn't want me to know." Ashlundt's face was contorted in pain. "Sara, I love you. You put the *curl* in my world. What more do you want me to say?"

She's too hurt to forgive him now. I thought, as I looked on.

Sara placed her hands on her hips in protest. "Do you call what you feel for me *love?* It's too much about you and what you need all the time, Ash. I just can't deal with you and your *needs* right now. I have to take care of myself for a change." She spun quickly on her heels and walked in the direction of the elevators, leaving Ashlundt still kneeling on the floor.

I barked out once as she breezed by me, hoping to get Sara's attention. It worked. She stopped in her tracks, turned back to me and bent down to give me a loving pat on the head. "Take care of him, boy," she whispered in my ear, then walked on and disappeared into the elevator.

I was feeling so confused. And here I thought we might finally all be going home together as a family. Instead, I had only Ashlundt to console. I trotted over to him and whined in sympathy as he stood slowly. He wiped his face with his hands, then took me by the collar. "Let's go home, boy. I guess I got what I deserved."

****

I couldn't let go of the empty feeling of Sara's absence. Every morning after our hospital visit, I would bring another one of my gentle reminders to Ashlundt. First it was the photograph. Then the bracelet. Finally, I pulled a left-behind pair of sweatpants of hers down from the open closet and laid it across his lap. In response, he picked up the phone and ordered up a dozen roses to be delivered to her at the medical center. Soon, no reminders were needed.

One long afternoon was spent at a gift store in Santa Monica. Ashlundt purchased a lot of sentimental cards and little gifts to send to Sara. One was a stuffed yellow lab that looked much like yours truly – particularly its stout build. He brought charms at a jewelry store for her charm bracelet, then spent the evening attaching them for her. He became relentless in his pursuit of her, trying to somehow make up for his neglect.

Ashlundt often tried calling Sara on her cell phone. The voice on the other end was Sara, but it wasn't live. It was the message she had prerecorded when she first got the phone. After a piercing tone, Ashlundt would leave a message each time, begging her for forgiveness. "Sara, I'm heartsick about my behavior. I think it's because I love you so much that I couldn't bear to see you in pain. I know I was wrong. Please, please forgive me." The next day: "Sara, I've rebuilt the practice. I did it for us, Sara, like you wanted me to. Please come home. We miss you."

We would often wait outside the medical center just to get a glimpse of her. It was always the same. She would kneel down to embrace me and ignore Ashlundt. One particular day he snuck up behind her while she was petting me, gently turned her by the shoulders and pushed the stuffed lab into her arms. "I know how much you miss Luke. I got this so you could have something to remind you of him," he whispered.

Sara was startled. Her instinct was to shove the plush doll back at him. Then, she paused, looked at it and took it from Ashlundt's trembling hands. She pulled it close to her chest and walked away. I barked after her, but she didn't turn around this time, not even for me.

****

Ashlundt set out on a campaign of calling Sara's friends. The first call was to Debi at her office. He caught her off-guard. "Debi, it's Ash. Please, don't hang up!"

"Ash, I'm not gonna talk to you about Sara. She's my friend, and I have no such loyalty to you after what you've done."

He leaned close to the speaker phone. "Look, I know. Beat me up all you want. But know this. I love Sara. I know that I've been wrong, but I want to help her. Not hurt her. Please, I just want to talk to her."

"Forget about it, Ash. And don't bother calling me again." She clicked off before he could say anything else.

Three more calls to other girlfriends went the same way. He begged them to intercede on his behalf. They all refused.

Then, an idea hit him. Dr. Wild. She was the veterinarian who had gotten close to Sara when they worked together at the pet clinic. His first call only yielded voice mail. But she returned his call that afternoon.

"Hi, Ash. How are you? What's up? Is Luke feeling good? Is Sara okay?"

"Suzi, hi. I'm okay. Luke's fine." He reached over and stroked my head. "He's more than that. He's great. But, I'm calling you about Sara. She's battling cancer."

"Yes, I was so sorry to hear what she's been going through. But she told me the other day that she's doing so much better." Dr. Wild's voice was full of hope.

"Did she tell you that we're not together anymore?" His anxiety seemed to increase, and he picked up a paper weight and shifted it from one hand to the other.

"Ash! No! She didn't put it to me that way. She just mentioned that she was staying with her old roommate in Westwood during her treatment at UCLA. I'm so sorry to hear that."

Wow! And just like that he got what he needed. Quickly, he jotted down the information on a yellow sticky pad. "Uh, right. It's easier for her to be close to the hospital, sick as she's been." Ashlundt put down the pen and played along.

"Well, I'm glad you cleared up the mystery of her disappearance."

He suddenly stood and started to pace. "So, Suzi, when I called you before, you really didn't know what was going on with Sara?"

"No, I really didn't talk to her until just recently, Ash. Why? She didn't try to hide her illness from you, did she?" Dr. Wild's honesty was always obvious.

Ashlundt stopped pacing and hesitated slightly before answering. "Yes, Suzi, she did. But that's in the past."

"Oh, my God! Do you think the two of you will get back together?" Again, Dr. Wild always got to the heart of any matter quickly.

"That's my hope, Suzi. That's my hope. Well, great talking to you. And, thanks."

"For what?"

"For being Sara's friend."

****

We were hiding in the bushes outside a small cottage-style house the very next night. Or, at least I thought that's what we were doing. Ashlundt told me in the car that this was in a small Westwood neighborhood near the UCLA campus. I wasn't sure what it all meant, but it hardly mattered. Outings were fun no matter where we went.

The front yard was surrounded by a white picket fence, and the air was full of perfume from the honeysuckle growing behind the bushes. I felt like we were on a stakeout, just like in the police movies he used to watch. Ashlundt had even brought us my favorite microwave popcorn to share. I felt Ashlundt's desperation at resorting to stalking Sara by hiding in the bushes outside her friend's house. I could tell my master's legs were starting to cramp as he crouched for what seemed like hours awaiting her. We finished the popcorn, and I decided to stretch out and take a nap. But, I couldn't sleep. I was so full of hope that Sara would finally come back to us. Then, I heard the latch on the front gate and felt Ashlundt tense up. He had spotted her. I sat up and almost let out a bark, almost, but Ashlundt quickly clamped his big hand over my snout to remind me to be quiet.

We watched as she dragged up the walkway to the front door. She looked exhausted. Her shoulder-strap purse seemed to weigh her down. Ashlundt had littered the small front porch with two dozen red roses, more stuffed animals, the framed picture of the two of them. He also had tied a red velvet box to my fancy silver collar, which he left on the bottom step.

Sara stopped in her tracks and sank to the front steps shaking her head. The first item she reached for was the velvet box. Sara opened it to find the newly adorned silver charm bracelet. She began to cry into her hands, her thin body shaking. I could barely contain myself. I wanted to run to her as I always had in the bathroom at home and comfort her. Only Ashlundt had held me back.

Together, we finally made our move. We stepped out of the bushes and hurried across the driveway in ten big leaps to where she was sitting at the top of the steps. I beat my human to her, as I always did. He'd never beat me in a footrace in my lifetime. My wet nose must have startled Sara, because she grabbed my head and buried her face into my furry neck. Ashlundt knelt beside us. He remained silent.

"Why are you doing all this, Ash? It feels like you're stalking me."

"Don't you know, Sara? I love you more than I can tell you. Listen: I'm a damned, selfish fool. I never wanted to hurt you, but… please let Luke and me support you through all this now. You don't need to keep working so hard while you're sick. Please take time to heal, to get better. Let us help you, please." His sad, shining eyes met hers.

I gave out a soft bark, hoping my encouragement would help things along. Sara kept quiet and kept her distance from Ashlundt. I moved between them, wagging my tail, but neither Sara nor Ashlundt would blink. They were locked in each other's appraising gazes. I took a step back, just as Sara finally found the words to speak.

"I really appreciate how much you care. Thank you for all of this. It's just… I'm getting ready to have reconstructive surgery… had to wait because we weren't sure if I'd need radiation too. And I still need to be monitored for the cancer." She scooted back from him and drew a deep breath.

"I understand. Or at least, I want to understand. But it really doesn't change how I feel about you, Sara, even if you still need treatment. Let me go through it with you. The only thing that matters is that we're together again." Ashlundt leaned closer to Sara, but stopped short of reaching out for her. "Luke's missed you so much. Somehow, I think he understands everything – what you were going through, what I went through. He wants us to be together and happy."

Ashlundt nodded in my direction. I stepped forward and nudged Sara's hands with my face. She responded by scratching that perfect spot right behind my ears.

"Sara, please don't make us wait any longer. Promise me you'll never leave me again," Ashlundt stretched his hands toward her with his palms turned upward. "After all, on top of everything else, we have a wedding to plan. Or… at least we used to before you went away. What do you say? Promise me you'll never leave me? Tell me you still want to marry me? Sickness, health, whatever. I just want to be here for you…"

She put her hand up as if to block him. "Listen, Ash. I didn't feel that I could be honest with you about being sick. I didn't think you could handle it on top of the lawsuit and how depressed you'd become. I tried so many times to tell you, but you weren't there for me. You were so closed off."

"Sara, I promise you I'll change. I can. Forgive me."

"Oh, Ash, I… I… what can I say to you? Sara smiled through her tears.

He gently took her hands in his. "Just say one word, say *yes.*"

"Yes," she answered in a low, shuddering voice. "But this is conditional. It goes against all I believe. But, I can't help it right now. I don't have the strength. You see, while it's true that I left you for a year, it was you who abandoned me emotionally. I do want to be with you always, but only with an assurance that you'll try not to lose touch with your emotions, or mine."

Ashlundt spread his arms wide and pulled Sara close. "You have my promise," he whispered in her ear. "I am yours, heart, mind and soul… for as long as you'll put up with me… and our big furry friend."

I was so happy that I ripped around Debi's front yard barking and tearing up patches of sod in the process. Soon, I began a bout of chasing my tail. However intuitive I might have been with human emotion, after all, I was still a dog. And if this momentous occasion was truly what it seemed to be, I had at last helped bring the two humans about whom I cared most back together.

Chapter Six

The Blending

I lost count of my evening meals trying to figure out how long it was from that day until they were married. Instead, I counted Sara's monthly checkups from the time after her surgery.

"Ash, I think we should wait until after my hair is thicker, more presentable. And preferably, when they say I'm cancer-free."

Sara sweated out every checkup before each appointment in the master bathroom with me. "Oh, Luke. I know I counsel my patients to face their fears… but… I'm… I have nightmares about the cancer coming back." She would always pull me close and sob out her fears to me.

"What if it comes back, boy? I can't handle it again."

Of course, I knew that it wasn't back; I couldn't smell it on her. I would lick her face and try to let her know that it was all right. Perhaps the most frustrating element of being a dog is the inability to verbalize important details the way humans do. We went through that eight times before Sara felt it safe to plan the wedding.

I'll never forget the day of her final appointment. That morning it was cool enough for me to take a nap in the car while she went in for her checkup. I was startled awake by her squeals of delight when she opened the door and grabbed me in the backseat!

"It's gone, Luke! It's gone! I'm free of the cancer!"

I covered her neck with wet kisses. She was so excited that she almost pulled me off the seat and into the parking lot. Instead, I jumped out and ran circles around her as she did a funny dance and kept yelling, "Yes! Yes! Yes!"

Suddenly she stopped in mid-dance as if an idea had seized her. "Okay, boy. Let's celebrate. Let's go to Dave's Bridal and look for a wedding dress!"

It was the first dress she tried. I sat staring at her as she stood before the long, three-way mirror in the large salon containing what seemed like miles of wedding apparel. She was almost manic with the sales lady about everything.

"Look, it's perfect!" She twisted in every direction to admire the dress. "I just got a clean bill of health! No more cancer. I think the surgeon did a good job on me. Does the strapless look all right?"

The saleswoman, the surrounding shoppers, no one could get a word in edge-wise. They all just smiled and nodded. She was a beautiful vision, and everyone knew it.

After one last look in the mirror, she knelt next to me and grabbed my face, pulling my nose close to hers. "Oh, Luke. Ash kept his promise. He's been so wonderful. Taken care of me like he said."

It was the perfect day, full of happiness for us. She had called Ashlundt four times on her cell phone to tell him the news. I could hear his excitement through the phone. "Thank God! You're free… we're free! Come home… now, my love; I want you… here with me! Yahoo!" He sounded like he was jumping up and down because his breath was coming out in spurts in between his words.

I couldn't believe it was finally going to happen. We were getting married!

We hurried home to find Ashlundt standing in the front yard waiting for us. The minute the Mini Cooper pulled into the driveway, he yanked open the door, pulled Sara out of the driver's seat and flung her round and round. Tim and Corky must have been tipped off, because they came rushing over. Corky immediately pushed everyone inside to the kitchen table and started rattling off ideas for the wedding.

"What about the backyard? It's beautiful. A tent…" Corky suggested.

Sara jumped up from her kitchen chair. "Perfect. That way no one'll complain about Luke being a part of the wedding party." She sat down again suddenly absorbed in thought. She picked up a shaker and poured salt through her fingers. "If we do that, though, we should wait until April. Hopefully it won't rain, and it'll be warm enough."

"But that's more than two months away, Sara." Ashlundt put a large hand over her still much too thin arm. "Do we have to wait that long?" Ashlundt looked at Tim with a shrug.

Corky smacked Ashlundt on the arm, "Well, it's gonna take us that long to get it all together! Men! You have no clue!"

The girls laughed, and the men decided a beer toast was in order.

The time flew by. Sara and Corky – who was now becoming Sara's stand-in mother – finalized all the plans.

****

They had the service in our backyard in a white tent. I was the *ring boy*. Sara had concocted a lacy pouch that tied to a very worthy new collar that she had bought for me in Beverly Hills. The old silver one had gotten a little worse for the wear with all the dragging around it had gone through. The new one was black with fancy rhinestones in it, and the pouch was white and decorated with smaller sparkles. It held their two rings. I had spent the morning at the groomer's and was the cleanest I'd ever been. I must say that I made quite a stir when I took to the aisle and carried out my part admirably.

When I got up to the canopy, I turned back and looked at the happy crowd. There was Ashlundt's large family from San Diego, Sara's friends from USC and UCLA, some of her closest cancer therapy patients, the staff of the vet clinic, Ashlundt's colleagues and all of the neighbors. All together, seventy-five humans attended.

The white tent was decorated with beautiful bunches of roses. A white runner went down the center, leading to two smaller columns topped with flowers. A minister in a white robe stood between them. White wooden chairs flanked either side of the aisle. Each end chair had a floral arrangement tied to it. A harpist and a cello player entertained the guests as they awaited the happy couple. The backyard was beautiful. Stone steps outlined by newly blooming flowers led to the tent. I checked everything out, then went to find Sara and Ashlundt in the master bedroom.

Sara looked radiant. Her hair, now grown out to just above her shoulders, was cut in stylish feathered layers around her face and left unadorned. I kept stepping on the long train of her strapless dress that revealed a most successful reconstruction of her chest. Sara laughed. "Luke! You're gonna pull this dress down around my waist. Hey, I'm thrilled that I have two breasts again, but we don't need to give our guests the whole picture!"

Sara turned to Ashlundt as they got dressed and smiled at him. "You look so handsome. Like a real fairytale groom."

Ashlundt had exchanged his usual surfer dude look for a handsome dark suit, crisp white shirt, a matching tie and handkerchief. I wish I could have seen colors to describe everything better. His hair was combed back away from his perpetually tan face. As I've told you before, Ashlundt was a tall man. I heard him tell his tailor that he was six foot four. Because Sara was such a tall woman, they made a striking couple standing there in front of the floor-length bedroom mirror together. Ashlundt smiled at her and reached over to kiss her on the cheek. "Sara, you take my breath away. Are you sure we aren't tempting bad luck by getting dressed together?"

"No way, buddy. You're stuck with me; get used to it!" she teased. She pinched his arm and laughed.

"Well, I know you didn't fall for me over my fashion sense. But what was it that drew you to me?" His eyes smiled back at her playfully.

"Honestly, Ash, I'll tell you what it was. It was the fact that you didn't give a fig that you spent $18,000 trying to save old Bear. That dog was your best friend as far as you were concerned. This showed me from the start what a wonderful heart you have."

Ashlundt smiled wistfully. "Yeah, Bear was my buddy. I couldn't lose him too, like what happened with Aaron. Thankfully you brought Luke into our lives, and now I have you both." He wrapped his arms snugly around her waist. "We have something else in common."

Sara placed her hands on Ashlundt's cheeks. "Really? And what would that be?" She was smiling brightly.

"Well, that day when I first met you at the clinic, you told me you didn't have a dog of your own because you were juggling school and work. You said it would break your heart to have one alone at home. Sara, that's exactly when I knew you were my kind of girl."

They embraced and looked into each other's eyes. A knock on the door interrupted and was followed by Corky's voice, "Okay, you two; it's time!"

"Come on, Luke," Ashlundt waved at me, "let's go!"

Tim gave the bride away, since she had no immediate family. Ashlundt's dad Asa was his best man. Sara's best friend Debi was her maid of honor, and Corky, Lauren and Stephanie were her bride's maids. A white and gold carriage pulled by four white horses took the newlyweds and me to the Clubhouse Reception at the Bell Canyon Equestrian Center. The guests all followed behind in their cars.

It was quite an affair. I particularly enjoyed the table scraps of roast veal and grilled chicken that the guests happily shared. That, and the white frosting from the wedding cake. Afterward, I lay on a satin pillow that Sara had made for me, next to the bridal party table. I watched the two of them dancing. I could see how they adored each other, how it affected the people around them. Everyone seemed drawn to them.

Ashlundt and Sara were beautiful together. All afternoon they seemed surrounded by a white glowing light. I watched them for a long time until the light became blurry images surrounded by a dark aura. I wiped at my eyes with my paws, but the image wouldn't change. In that moment, a feeling of dread permeated my entire body. I began to shake, my tail wagging uncontrollably. Something was very wrong. On the one hand, I had felt so proud all that day that I'd been able in a small way to bring them together again. But, it wasn't over. I didn't know how, where or when, but I just knew I wasn't finished helping them yet.

Luke's Tale

Chapter Seven

The Fading

I was gratified to have witnessed the beginning of their love, but regretful that I had to see their pain. So many humans seem oblivious to the pain of others until they have felt it themselves. Oddly, it was even easier for me to *feel* their emotions when I started to go blind.

It began at their wedding; I kept seeing halos around Ashlundt and Sara. Soon, my vision became blurry. I sometimes felt like I had grains of sand in my eyes. No matter how hard I tried to wipe it away by rubbing my face on the carpet or into my bed, it wouldn't stop. My peripheral vision, as the doctor called it, seemed to be reduced, and I started bumping into furniture and losing my balance on steps. Ashlundt noticed right away.

"Come here, boy. Let me look at you." He placed his hands on both sides of my face and peered into my eyes. "Sara," he called as he released my face and stood, "I don't see anything wrong with Luke's eyes, but something's going on. Let's take him to Suzi."

The next thing I knew, Sara and Ashlundt had loaded me into the SUV and I was off to the vet. I never loved going on that trip – no dog does – but I knew there was something that needed to be done to fix my worsening problem.

"What do you think is wrong?" Sara asked as Ashlundt took the back streets to Chatsworth.

"I don't know, but it isn't normal. He's been bumping around for several weeks. I've been keeping an eye on him."

Ashlundt reached back to me and tweaked my left ear with his fingers. "It's been worrying me."

"I've noticed that he doesn't seem to see well at night when I take him out before bedtime, but it just didn't click with me that something was wrong," Sara reached back to scratch me under my chin. "We've been so lucky with him. He's not even four yet. I hope it's nothing serious."

Even though I didn't relish the exam part of going to the clinic, I loved seeing the people there. The clinic was a funny round building – almost a landmark in Chatsworth. A semi-circular grassy lawn with lots of shrubs flanked the backside of it, and I had probably marked every piece of greenery on it. The building had a very sterile smell to it that made my nose twitch. But the people were warm and always had a peanut butter treat for me.

Dr. Suzi Wild was standing at the front counter when we entered. A small, slim woman with short blonde hair and dark brown eyes, she has a quiet strength about her that was very reassuring to her patients. Even though she was a good friend to my humans, she was always the utmost professional when in the clinic. She knelt down and gave me a good scratch behind my ear, then took my leash and guided me back to the exam room.

An assistant named Hector lifted me onto a metal exam table. Dr. Wild gave me a soothing massage on my head and looked into my eyes intently. "Okay, boy, I'm going to give you a complete eye exam."

She walked over to a counter and picked up a funny-looking object and placed it on her head. "This is an ophthalmoscope, boy. It has a light and a lot of magnification so I can see what's going on in your eyes. Hold still."

She leaned close to me and shined the light in my eyes. Ugh! I didn't like it and tried to move my head, but Hector had both this hands on the sides of my ears. She drew closer to me, and I could see a hole in the middle of the strange object. She finally turned off the light and removed the instrument after what seemed like forever. "Oh, Luke, I've got some bad news for your mom and dad."

The tone in her voice alarmed me, but I knew she had figured out what was wrong.

70

After my check-up, Ashlundt, Sara and I sat together and waited for Dr. Wild's diagnosis. I was enjoying all the extra love and attention they both heaped on me when the vet joined us.

"Ash. Sara. I have bad news, you two. We can confirm this with a veterinary ophthalmologist, but I'm fairly sure that it's progressive retinal atrophy or PRA."

"Oh, no." Sara gasped and jumped up from her kneeling position next to me.

"What? What is it?" Ashlundt stood from his chair next to the exam table.

"We had other cases of it when I worked here." Sara took Ashlundt's hand.

"It isn't life-threatening, but, as Sara knows, it'll affect his vision. PRA is a genetic disease seen in Labs and a few other breeds. Basically, it's the degeneration of the retina. It causes ongoing vision loss... and... ultimately blindness." She stepped toward me and patted my back gently as I stood to meet her hand.

Blind. I was going blind? It made sense, but I suddenly wasn't capable of rational thought. The fear of what I had just learned overtook my entire body, and I began to shake. *What was going to happen to me?*

"Blindness? Luke, blind? How can that be?" Ashlundt rubbed his forehead. "Is this treatable?"

"You didn't do anything to cause this, Ash. The condition in nearly all breeds is inherited as a recessive trait. There's no treatment; not even surgery. PRA is similar to retinitis pigmentosa in humans." The vet pointed to her own eyes. "Eventually as the disease progresses, he'll most likely develop cataracts."

"But, I bought him from the best of breeders. I can't imagine that George Brown would breed dogs with genetic defects." Ashlundt's voice was angry and disappointed.

Dr. Wild looked downward and rubbed her forehead. "I can't address that, as I don't really know much about Luke's breeder. But you and Sara, you'll need to decide if you're prepared to have the responsibility of a blind dog."

"Of course we are!" Ashlundt declared, pounding the metal exam table next to him for emphasis. The loud noise startled me. "I hope you aren't suggesting that we put him down over loss of his sight?"

"No, of course not." The vet knelt down next to me, looked into my eyes and stroked my forehead. "But blind pets; they're a big responsibility. He will be blind and dependent upon you to teach him how to cope with it and get around."

"Sounds like that could be tricky," Sara chimed in as she sat down on the floor and pulled me closer. "Is that really as hard as it sounds?"

Dr. Wild smiled and took Sara's hand in hers. "Actually, PRA dogs, they can be quite resourceful. They have an uncanny way of learning their surroundings and dealing with their blindness. Some people don't have the patience to allow them to learn how to be blind. I didn't think that was the case with either of you, but I just had to let you know." The vet released Sara's hand.

Ashlundt joined the three of us on the floor. "Don't worry, Suzi; Luke is part of our family. We love him. We'll help him get through this." Ashlundt threw his arms around me and rested his head on my back. Sara reached over to me and held my front paws in a show of affection. It was comforting to know that I wasn't being abandoned by the people I loved. Especially for some strange condition that had me feeling scared, confused and downright depressed.

****

It was Sara who first guided me through it all. Even in the midst of a full load of therapy with cancer patients, plus her continuing doctoral program at UCLA, she found the time to work with me.

My vision of the world faded away slowly. Some days I could still see shapes, objects and specs of light. Other days, when the sun was very bright, or if there was lots of light in a room, I could see fairly well – even make out people's expressions. At other times I would only see shadows where people and things once stood. I felt both scared and angry that this was happening to me. But Sara was vigilant in preparing me for a day when the lights would go out forever. During every break that she had, she would cover my eyes with a blindfold to block out all light to help me "practice" being blind. She wore an ankle chain with bells to help me know where she was at all times. She didn't need it. I could smell her scent of fresh cut flowers anywhere.

We started by mapping out the house, the backyard, and then later our neighborhood and the trails. On the days when she was swamped with work, she would have our neighbor Corky walk with me through my new routine of learning my environment blindfolded. Ashlundt probably would have helped if he weren't so busy with patients.

Sara did all she could to help me get my bearings. She even got down on all fours so she could see and remove obstacles, like cactus plants with sharp needles, or other plants with pointy stalks that might harm me at my level. She taught me help words like *stop, step up, step down, easy, slow, careful* and *danger.* I surprised her when she tried out directions like *right* and *left* on me. Most dogs have difficulty understanding the concept of *right* and *left,* but I guess I was an exception. I learned it some time ago from watching the trainers with their students and horses at the equestrian center with Sara. The trainer would tell the rider to turn left and then turn right, and I would watch the direction in which the student would turn the horse. I understood and obeyed from the very minute that she directed me to turn right, then turn left. "What a smart boy you are!" Her praise was always followed by a hug and a peanut butter cookie.

Sara would let me know when she was walking out of a room, or approaching to touch me when I was sleeping or relaxed. She talked to me constantly, even with silly chatter that I enjoyed, like "Lukey, what a big brave boy!" or "You're so good, I'm going to eat you up!" And then she would sit down on the floor, pulling me into her lap and rubbing her face into my neck like she was going to gobble me down. I loved being her good boy.

I tried to return the favor by comforting her before each of her continuing cancer checkups and scans. Even though she had been declared cancer-free, Ashlundt had insisted that she have consistent follow-up. It had become a ritual for us to sit in the bathroom, my head in her lap, while she talked out all her dread of going to the oncologist.

"Luke, I'm terrified that it'll come back. How can I go through it again?" She would rock back and forth and wipe her eyes with toilet tissue. I would snuggle closer to comfort her, but I always knew that it hadn't returned.

She took me with her to her appointments, and the receptionist would always protest my presence. "Hey, no dogs allowed!"

Sara was adamant. She would stare at the woman with her hands on hips. "I'm sorry that you don't like dogs, but he's my security blanket. I need him to be here with me."

I would always sit in the waiting room between the comfortable, overstuffed chairs, making myself small so as not to draw attention, or cause a problem during her exams. And, I felt her relief each time she came out of the exam area with a clean bill of health. "It's okay, boy! It's okay. Let's go celebrate and get you a hot dog!"

I would jump for joy at both Sara's good news and her tasty suggestion.

Sara continued to "blind proof" the house so I wouldn't get hurt. She removed or covered sharp edges from tables or cabinets that were eye-level with me. She tried to teach me how to carefully take stairs, especially up to Tim and Corky's house, but I figured it out quickly. I knew them too well by memory. Sara even put carpet squares at the entrance of every doorway so I would know that I was entering a room. She bought me eye-shields for our long walks and play sessions so I wouldn't bump into sharp twigs or low growing shrubs. She bought me scented balls and Frisbees to enhance our play sessions. This all just confirmed how unconditional her love for me had become. She was giving back to me what I had always given to her. I would have willingly given my life for her if she needed it.

Then, she gave me the ultimate gift. After dinner one night as we all lounged on the sofa in the den, Sara handed some pamphlets to Ashlundt.

"Ash, I've been thinking. Helping others is therapeutic."

"Yes, I agree." He seemed to be listening with one ear as he scanned one of his journals.

"I experienced it with my own cancer, and in providing therapy for other cancer patients."

"Where are you going with this, love?" He put down his publication and turned his full attention to her.

"I've decided that Luke should become a therapy dog."

I perked up at the mention of my name and listened intently.

"Hmmn. Why do you think so?" Ashlundt put his arm around her.

"Well, he meets all the behavioral requirements listed in the brochure. He has an outstanding temperament. He tolerates other animals well. He really loves people and children." She became increasingly animated, pushing her once-again long hair behind her ears.

I began to beat my tail against the leather couch in agreement. This sounded like fun.

Ashlundt took one of the pamphlets and examined it. "This says he needs to be up-to-date on all his vet checkups and vaccinations, and also be over a year old. He's okay with all of that. But I don't have time to do it." He pulled at her denim shirt playfully.

"Not you, silly. Me. I'd be the handler."

"Like you have time, Sara?"

"Ash, you make time for what's important to you." Sara reached down and patted me gently on top of my head.

He smiled and kissed her on the check. "Sounds like a plan." With that he immediately returned to his journal. Sara rested her head on his shoulder and watched TV with my head in her lap.

We joined *Therapy Dogs International* the next day. I sat with her in her office while she read about the organization out loud to me. "It says that TDI was formed in New Jersey in 1976. Wow! 21,000 dogs nationwide are registered with them. They have a big branch right here in Ventura and another in Los Angeles."

I thumped my tail in approval.

"Says here that they provide qualified volunteer handlers and their *therapy dogs* for visits to hospitals and nursing homes. They provide training and testing programs." With that she dialed their number.

****

We were asked to meet a man named Jack Champion in the Chatsworth Park at ten o'clock on a Saturday morning. There were five other dogs waiting when we arrived. One German Shepherd was so aggressive and unruly. He was barking and baring his teeth at everyone who passed by. I knew he didn't have a snowball's chance to pass.

We sat on the grass and watched the others all go through the evaluation before us. It was really all about temperament and obedience. Because the Shepherd was so out of control, Jack

Champion told his teenaged owner, a girl with pigtails and braces, to leave right away. It was admirable that she wanted to volunteer, but the Shepherd had no manners.

Next a Labradoodle named Neo was introduced to Champion. He shook hands and sat up for the evaluator. He was obviously a real sweetheart. His middle-aged male owner was given all the paperwork to prepare for training and testing. Two others – a female Cocker Spaniel named Miss Brown and a Dobie named Lucky tried to pick a fight with each other. They were sent packing as well. Another well-behaved yellow Lab named Simon and his female owner passed and got their papers.

Finally, it was our turn. Sara took me off leash, and I walked by her side to Mr. Champion and sat in front of him. "Hello, uh, Mrs. Jaynes. This must be… Luke. Hi, Luke!"

I immediately sat up and offered my right paw.

"Good dog," he said as he shook my offered paw. "Does he have any bad habits? Ever bite anyone? Aggressive for any reason?"

"No, no and no." Sara was sounding confident in my good behavior tendencies.

"Walk with him please," Mr. Champion instructed.

We walked about fifteen feet away from him, then turned back. I paused for a moment, distracted by a bunch of crows dive-bombing a tree. I'd have to be completely blind to have missed that. After all, Labs are bird dogs.

"Luke, forward," Sara whispered.

"Does he like meeting people? Can he tolerate loud noises? Disruptions? React compassionately to people crying?" Mr. Champion was leaning forward on his tall stool.

This time Sara responded "yes" to all questions."

He reached down and petted me on the head. "Nice dog, Mrs. Jaynes. Your application says he has PRA, but obviously not enough to distract him from the birds. I'm impressed." He handed Sara the necessary paperwork and an instruction manual. "Use this to get him ready for the testing. Date, time and location are on the front. Next testing is in two weeks, but there's a testing schedule attached, and you can go to any of them in either L.A. or Ventura."

"That's all you need to see?" Sara seemed confused.

"This evaluation is just to see if he has the temperament to be a therapy dog. He does." Mr. Champion smiled, picked up his stool and headed for his car, leaving us to enjoy the park for a while longer.

****

I wasn't in the least bit nervous the day of our test. Sara had fully prepared me. She explained that the test evaluates if a dog is sensitive and attentive to people. Obviously I had to be their guy. Lots of dogs provide love and companionship in a home, but not all of them have the temperament suited to be a therapy dog.

I sat while Sara pulled on her favorite jeans, a dressy top and a fancy black belt. A new pair of black leather boots completed her look. She brushed her hair that cascaded down her back while I grabbed my good collar and leash. We were off.

Sara drove us to a building in Ventura, an ocean-side town about forty minutes north of our home in Bell Canyon. It was located in a small, ordinary-looking warehouse that Sara said was provided by volunteers, since TDI worked on a shoe-string budget. A makeshift waiting room had been set up with uncomfortable looking folding chairs just inside the warehouse entrance. We waited our turn for the two main evaluators to work their way through testing six other dogs. Sara seemed nervous while we waited, but I knew it was gonna be a piece of cake, as she would sometimes say. That comment always made me hungry.

We sat for what Sara said was an hour. The warehouse was large and appeared to have different areas where various dogs were being run through types of tests. There was white masking tape stuck to the floor in different areas. I decided not to watch the other dogs. I was rather content to just take a nap.

"Luke and Sara Jaynes?" A male voice called out from behind a desk. This alerted me that it was our turn. A short, thin, gray-haired man in khaki pants and a white shirt with a green TDI vest approached me and gave me a friendly pet on my back. I wagged my tail, sat quietly and watched him intently.

"Hello, Mrs. Jaynes, I'm Evan Sanders with TDI. I see your dog is very friendly." He smelled like coffee, but had a very kind voice. He then shook hands with Sara.

He escorted us over to a table with metal objects lying on top of it. From a distance, I couldn't quite make out what they were. I wagged my tail even harder when Sara put gentle pressure on my leash. It was her signal to me that it was time to sit quietly next to her, just as we had practiced.

Mr. Sanders reached around to the table behind him and threw a bed pan on the concrete floor. It made a loud smack. I stared at the metal object curiously. It made no movement. He checked something on the clipboard that he was carrying, then said, "Very good, Luke." He looked up and smiled at Sara. "He stays calm in surprising situations. That's good."

"Yes, he's very calm," Sara added nervously.

We moved to the next "station." It was a small area sectioned off with pipe and drape and set up with medical equipment. Mr. Sanders instructed, "Please walk him around the wheelchair and then around the woman standing behind the walker."

Sara moved forward, and I followed. "Okay. Luke come." We walked around an empty wheelchair that was sitting in the center of the area. Next, we stepped around an older woman leaning on the walker. She was dressed in a light-colored sweat suit. I gave the woman a curious glance. She appeared bored.

Again, Mr. Sanders checked off something on his clipboard. "Very good. Some dogs don't do well around medical equipment."

"Good boy, Luke!" Sara exclaimed. She gave me an encouraging rub on the ear.

"Mrs. Jaynes, Luke's done pretty well so far. Test Three demonstrates how well Luke will welcome being groomed and examined by others. It also verifies whether or not he will permit a stranger to touch him." The evaluator began to brush me with his hand, then lightly examined my ears and each front foot. I enjoyed his touch. I wagged my tail and smiled at him. I was breathing heavily through a wide open-mouthed smile.

"Nicely done, Luke." He patted me on the back, then looked up to Sara. "My examination also reveals your care and sense of responsibility for his grooming, Mrs. Jaynes."

I was confident from my earlier bath that I was making a good showing. Actually, I smelled quite nice if I don't say so myself. Of course, I'd much rather have bathed in gravy or a tub of melted cheese that morning. However, for the purposes of this exam, the No-More Tears shampoo sufficed.

"He gets a weekly bath, Mr. Sanders." Sara still seemed nervous and kept pushing her hair behind her ears.

Once again, he checked off something on the clipboard. I could hear the squeak of his pen against the smooth paper.

"Okay, now take Luke for a walk the length of the room, please."

I walked on Sara's left side. Sara whispered "Good boy" under her breath.

"Turn left, then right and then do an about turn. Stop in between each movement and then at the end, please," he ordered. Mr. Sander's voice grew louder as we moved further away from him. His voice echoed off the walls of this big room.

I easily anticipated our moves and sat as soon as we stopped. I was able to see fairly well because the warehouse had really strong, bright lights. I could make out that Mr. Sanders smiled at this one.

"I'm impressed, Mrs. Jaynes. Even though I didn't ask Luke to sit at the end, he did. That's the sign of a highly-trained dog."

"Thank you." Sara smiled back at him.

"Okay, now put him on a stay, please," Mr. Sanders requested. That was easy. It meant that I could sit or lie down but remain in place without moving. Sara did as she was asked, and I obeyed by sitting and then lying down. Nothing terribly complicated.

"Now walk away from him the entire length of the room, please." Mr. Sanders pointed at Sara, then motioned with his hand for her to move away from me.

I did my best to follow her with my eyes. She grew fuzzier to me as she moved farther away. However, I didn't move another muscle until she called out, "Luke, come!" That's when I leaped up and ran quickly to the location from where her voice was emanating, again sitting when I reached Sara's side. This was so easy. We did all this when Ashlundt and Sara took me through puppy training. It's the sort of thing that a dog never forgets.

As I sat next to her, another handler, a friendly middle-aged woman named Jane, and her dog approached us from a distance.

Jane stopped, introduced herself and shook hands with Sara. As they chatted, Jane's large Great Dane towered over me and made me feel like a dwarf. He was quite handsome with a large head and short brindle coat. His name was Zack, and he was quite excited. However, I showed no more than a casual interest in him. If I was being tested, I didn't want to mess it up by roughhousing with another dog. Whatever I did – or didn't do – it seemed to work. Again, a squeaky checkmark.

"Okay, Mrs. Jaynes. Walk Luke past the food bowl over at the far side of the room."

Food! That got my full attention. At last, a task that I could possibly enjoy. I tried my best to keep my tongue from hanging out of my mouth. As we drew nearer, I could smell the mouth-watering beefy contents of the bowl. My stomach growled. I went for it! Sara immediately jerked on my leash. "No, Luke! Leave it!" I hung my head in shame. What can I say? I thought it was mealtime.

Sara was upset with me, muttering under her breath, "Leave the food, Luke."

We walked slowly back to Mr. Sanders. I saw him making a notation on his clipboard.

"Okay. Not so good with the food, but well done on the rest," Mr. Sanders said aloud.

"But will he be exposed to bowls of food on the floor in a hospital, Mr. Sanders?" Sara's agitation was obvious.

"No worries, Mrs. Jaynes. Therapy dogs don't visit during mealtime. Very few Labs ever pass that test on the first try. We'll do it again in a moment."

"Oh, I see." Sara breathed a sigh of relief.

"Mrs. Jaynes, I don't normally do this, but I need to excuse myself for a brief restroom break. We've been at this for hours, and my coffee is catching up with me. Do you mind?"

"No, of course not. I'll take Luke outside for a break. We'll be back in five."

We headed outside. There appeared to be not a single patch of grass anywhere near the concrete parking lot. We walked around the circumference of the building. Finally, a small patch of crab grass at the end of the pavement next to a loading dock. I lifted a hind leg to relieve myself. Sara reached for her phone and tried to call Ashlundt.

"Damn, voice mail. I wanted to let him know how great you're doing, Luke. He's probably with a patient."

Mr. Sanders greeted Sara as we reentered the warehouse through a back door. "Oh, there you are! Would you let me take your dog for a while?"

"Um, is this part of the test? I didn't see it in the training." Sara was apprehensive. She seemed to pull a little tighter on my leash.

"No, but we like to throw a few curve balls when a dog is this good, Mrs. Jaynes. Aside from the food temptation, he's almost too good to be true."

"And that's bad because...?"

"It's not bad. Just want to see how he'll behave in your absence. Hypothetically speaking, let's say you have to go to the restroom while Luke's with a patient at a hospital. How will he react when you're not around?"

"Oh, I see. But Luke has PRA. Eventually he's gonna go blind. He's coping with that, and I don't like to leave him alone. So, I wouldn't just abandon him in the middle of a session."

Sanders scribbled something on his chart.

"Will that impede his acceptance into the program? I know you don't accept deaf dogs, but what about blind dogs?" Now Sara was sounding concerned.

"Actually, I would never want you to leave Luke alone with a patient. That was part of the test."

"Oh... I see." Sara sighed in relief, then let out a nervous giggle. "Trick question, I guess."

"Ms. Jaynes, you were forthcoming in your application. I think Luke will inspire patients with his blindness. No problem on the PRA."

Whew! Other people who accepted my blindness. That was a relief, I thought to myself.

Mr. Sanders took a couple of steps toward us. "Oh, hey, let's try the food bowl again, shall we? Walk him over to it."

Sara tugged gently on my leash for me to follow her. I smelled the meat again and my mouth began to water. We drew closer. Sara's tugging grew more firm. She kept whispering,

"Leave it, Luke. Leave it!" I got the message. This time, I took in the aroma but didn't rush the bowl. It took more than a little effort on my part. I clenched my teeth tightly and swallowed hard. *I'm a vegetarian*, I tried convincing myself for a half minute. We walked calmly past it, turned around and headed back to Sanders.

"Better. Much better," Mr. Sander's declared with a smile.

"Good dog, Luke." Sara reached into her coat pocket and pulled out a Charlie Bear, one of my favorite snacks. This time, it wasn't a food tease. She tossed it in the vicinity of my snout. I snatched it in mid-air and chomped it to smithereens.

"Good maneuvering on your part, Mrs. Jaynes." Mr. Sanders was smiling. "He responds well to you. Let's go out back for his final test."

We followed Saunders through some double doors to a vacant lot behind the warehouse. Little boys in jeans, t-shirts and tennis shoes were playing baseball in a make-shift ball field. Young girls in shorts and tank tops had drawn hop-scotch on the concrete and alternated between that and jump rope. Others were just sitting quietly on blankets playing with dolls or trucks.

I wanted to run and play with them so badly that I could barely contain my wagging tail again. Sara, however, stood quietly by the metal doors. I took my cue from her and sat quietly by her side as she gestured me to do.

"I know that he would go over and start playing with them if he could, Mrs. Jaynes, and he would be a great playmate. But we can't allow him to be physically near them. I can see by his reaction that he likes children."

Sara didn't respond. I think she was still worried about the food bowl incident.

Mr. Sanders patted me on the head. "Luke, Mrs. Jaynes, follow me back inside please."

We walked back through the double doors and over to the registration table in the front of the warehouse. Sanders grabbed materials off the table and turned to Sara, "Congratulations. You and Luke will receive your credentials in a few weeks. After that, you can start your visits. I need to take both your photos for your ID cards."

We were taken into an office through a doorway in the back of the room. First, Sara stood in front of a plain white wall and positioned her feet between a pair of black lines on the tile floor. She smiled naturally at a man holding a camera on a tripod. A flashbulb went off. I think she blinked a little, but perhaps that was me reacting to the bright popping of light. Next, Sara had me hop up on a wooden table, maybe three feet off the ground. There were a couple of white lines in the center made with masking tape. Sara helped position me between the lines, then took a step back. "Good boy, Luke. Just sit." Another pop of light occurred. I was so out of sorts from the first flashbulb that I didn't even see the photographer taking my picture.

Mr. Sanders must have entered the room during the photo shoot. I heard him talking to Sara from the doorway.

"Luke is exactly the kind of dog we need in this program. Here are the instructions for you to order both your TDI vests and identification cards."

"Great. Thanks. I always wanted one of those vests." Sara sounded happy. "And, how will we set up our hospital visits? Do I need to call you?"

"Not me," Sanders answered. "You'll need to call and register with the hospitals and nursing homes in your area; get schedules from them for visits. It's all in your paperwork."

"Well, thank you, Mr. Sanders, for giving us this opportunity. We're both pretty excited to get started."

"Thank you, Sara." Mr. Sander's extended a hand, and Sara shook it. "And thanks for your willingness to have both of you serve. I know you'll both do great. Just keep big Luke away from the hospital cafeteria." He laughed as he departed. I barked in protest. I wasn't sure what a cafeteria was, but it sure sounded like a place I'd want to visit.

On the way to the car, I got the scooties, running around in big circles with my butt tucked under me. I had been a good boy for too long. I ran around and around the parking lot. Sara laughed hysterically at my antics. "Good thing Mr. Sanders can't see you now!"

Chapter Eight

The Therapy

Sara couldn't wait to tell Ashlundt the good news. We burst straight into his home office. "Honey, we did it! Luke's a therapy dog!"

Ashlundt looked up from behind his desk and flashed her a toothy smile. "Congratulations," he offered in a low voice and patted me on the head. "Good job, Luke."

"Yes, it's exciting. We practiced a whole lot to make this happen. And you should have seen Luke. You would've been so proud. He was perfectly obedient... well except for when they put the food out." She danced around me in a display of happiness.

Ashlundt laughed at that. "Luke's such a chow hound. He probably gets it from me."

Sara seemed anxious to tell him more, but he had already gone back to organizing some paperwork.

"Hey, don't you want to hear all about it?" She moved closer to his desk. "I tried to call you. What's so important you can't talk to us for a minute?"

Ashlundt dropped a stack of pages on his desk, then looked back up at Sara. "Sorry. Just need to finish up this new client interview. You can tell me about it at dinner, okay?"

I had begun to notice that Ashlundt seemed somewhat distracted once in a while again. It didn't make much sense to me. He and Sara were now happily together. Ashlundt's practice was back to being busy. I couldn't understand his occasional uneven behavior. I hoped everything was all right.

Sara shrugged it off and took me out for a rewarding long walk in the woods. I worried as we left, but then was soon distracted by the smells and sounds of the forest.

****

Our identification cards and vests arrived in the mail fifteen evening meals later. Sara signed me up with Northridge Hospital, a short drive from our house, for our initial visit. "Just twenty minutes from here, Lukey," Sara assured me. As if I was counting.

The next morning, Sara gave me a thorough scrubbing with baby shampoo so that I would look and smell my best. I didn't realize this was going to be part of the deal before each visit, but I guessed there had to be good and bad with any job.

I was a little nervous as we drove to the hospital that afternoon for my first day. I wanted to help sick people, just like Ashlundt had helped Sara get better when she was recovering from her surgery. I hoped I could do a good job and make people happy. But unlike Ashlundt, I couldn't cook people breakfast, do their laundry or dispense their medication. What tasks lay ahead for me were unclear.

We parked in the visitor parking lot and went into the newly redecorated facility. I could smell the fresh glue holding up the new wallpaper. The scent of newly installed carpet was overpowering. The lobby was decorated with real plants and had a large painting of an angel as we entered. A lot of men and women were sitting in leather chairs. One woman appeared to be showing her husband a small Teddy Bear that she'd found in the gift shop. It made me think of my bear at home. I wished I'd brought it to show the sick people in the hospital. We were directed to an office on the ground floor.

The TDI administrator at the hospital was a warm and vivacious redhead who read our nametags, then introduced herself. "Luke. Sara. Hi, I'm Rita. Thanks for visiting." She immediately pulled a Milk Bone treat from her apron pouch and tossed it straight into my mouth. She was all right in my book.

Sara and I were led to a nurses' station to get our room assignments for visitations that day. "The nurses always make the recommendations on who the therapy dogs should visit," Rita told Sara. A trio of older nurses stopped by at the desk. They seemed to be immediately taken with me. I got a lot of loving… and even a teaspoon of peanut butter! I was going to like this job.

Four patients were suggested for visits that first day. The first was Victor, a little boy who had sustained two broken legs and other multiple injuries in a car accident. We peeked inside the room. His legs were in casts, and he squirmed in great discomfort. His young mother was by his bedside trying to soothe him. When he saw me, his mouth broke into a huge grin.

"Hi, Victor." Sara stepped up to Victor's bedside. "This is Luke. He's here to visit with you. Do you like dogs?"

Victor laughed and smiled "Yes!"

Sara pushed a chair next to the bed and told me to sit in it. I climbed up next to Victor so that he could pet me, but he wasn't able to reach my body. His legs were suspended in an upright position. He just couldn't move over far enough to his left.

Turning to Victor's mother, Sara asked, "Would it be all right if I put a sheet on the bed so that Luke can lie next to him? He'd be much easier to reach."

"Absolutely," the mother consented. "Just be careful. He's very uncomfortable."

Sara ducked into a large closet in the corner of the room. She returned moments later with a folded white sheet. She spread it out on the bed and patted the sheet. I gently crawled next to him so he could wrap his arms around me. I was a little nervous that even the slightest nudge in the wrong direction might hurt this injured boy. I needn't have worried.

"Wow! That is amazing," his mother hugged herself in excitement. He's been here for three weeks. Been so miserable 'til now. That's the first time he's smiled since he woke up from the accident."

I felt the boy's happiness at having me to distract his pain. I quietly licked his hands, and Victor giggled constantly murmuring, "Furry doggie. Good boy."

Sara was right; helping others was definitely going to help me cope with my impending blindness. If just my mere presence could make this boy with broken legs so happy, it seemed the possibilities were endless.

We stayed with him for thirty minutes until a nurse walked in to administer Victor's pain medication. "C'mon, Luke. Time to go," Sara prodded. It was time to move on to the next patient.

We rode up in a crowded elevator to the fifth floor. This group of rooms had very different kinds of people inside. These folks weren't injured like Victor. They were suffering from a variety of serious illnesses. Illnesses I could smell from the moment the elevator doors opened.

We entered room 509. There was a woman sitting up in bed, watching *The Price Is Right* on TV. I knew that show well because the host, Bob Barker, was always saying something about spaying and neutering your pets at the end of the show. Ouch! I wasn't his biggest fan, but then again, I wasn't here to watch TV.

"Luke, this is Betty," Sara said. "Be gentle with her. She has a very aggressive form of Multiple Sclerosis." Sara then turned to the grey haired woman and asked if she wanted company. The woman immediately began to cry.

"I'm sorry. I'm in so much pain. Can't move my entire right side. Feels like my arm and leg are on fire, but please bring him closer."

"Would you like for him to lie next to you on the bed?"

"Yes, please. That would really help."

Sara again went to a corner closet and returned with a white sheet. After it was in place next to Betty on the bed, she positioned me with the patient, placing my head on her left shoulder. Her tears soon faded to smiles. "He's so beautiful and kind."

I didn't know it then, but this was actually my first of many visits to Betty over the course of several months. As her illness got worse, she lost even her ability to smile. Tears of joy would be the only clue I had that she was glad to see me.

My head is filled with stories of that first day. The little girl who was crying in agony until I sat with her and let her groom me with her hair brush. The bald teenaged boy who had been rushed to the hospital because of a bad reaction to his chemotherapy. I sat next to him in a chair and caught a small rubber ball in my mouth over and over. I walked away that day understanding what Sara meant about how helping others would be therapy for me. I was born to do this.

We started to go every Thursday afternoon to visit patients in various hospitals. One day at Northridge, Sara told me we were going to meet an elderly patient named Julia. When we entered the brightly lit room, I could see an elderly woman with white silver hair sitting in a wheel chair. She smelled of lilacs. Many of her friends surrounded her. One was a handsome elderly gentleman in a three-piece suit. Another was a middle-aged woman in a sweat suit that resembled the patient. Perhaps, she was a daughter. Another was a younger woman in jeans and a blouse. I thought perhaps a granddaughter.

Sara and I approached Julia, and Sara began talking. "Hello, Julia. This is Luke. He's a Labrador Retriever and a therapy dog. Would you like him to visit with you today?"

"No, go away!" She spat at us. "Don't touch me."

She wouldn't let me near her. I felt confused and didn't know what I'd done to offend her.

"I'm sorry." Sara nodded in apology. "We'll go."

We left, but I kept thinking about Julia all week. *Why was Julia mad at me? Why didn't she want to meet me? Had I done something wrong?* On our next visit, I hoped we could try again, but instead the hospital staff asked us to pay a visit to the Emergency Room. One of the nurses kept calling it "the ER."

I was surprised at how small the waiting room was. About twenty chairs lined the walls with two rows of seats back-to-back in the middle of the room. Every one of them was occupied. People were coughing, holding their heads or running back and forth to the bathroom. One older woman with her hand wrapped in a bloody cloth was surrounded by three children. The air was full of concern and fear. The nurse attendant at the registration counter asked us to wait so that she could get a list of beds for us to visit in the medical area. But, before she could return, I was quickly surrounded by the three young children, a boy and two girls, who had accompanied their grandmother.

"Hey, what's your dog's name, lady?"

"His name is Luke. He's a therapy dog. What are your names?" Sara asked in a soothing voice.

"I'm Diesel." The boy looked about six and had dark hair and freckles. He smelled like a playground full of sand.

"I'm Laurel." The taller girl looked to be about eight and had long blonde hair and beautiful light eyes. She smelled of bubble gum. She took a comb out of her pocketbook and started grooming me while popping off pink bubbles.

"My name's Munchie. I like doggies." This from a short three-year-old girl with sandy hair and dark eyes. She smelled of urine and baby powder. She joined her sister in the grooming process, though she was a bit rough on my tail. I wanted to bark at her to stop yanking, but I didn't want to startle all the kids. Instead, I just wagged my tail and licked their hands.

"Grandma cut herself while she was making lunch. Her finger is bleeding," Diesel explained. "Wrapped it up with one of Munchie's old diapers."

"Oh, no!" Sara exclaimed. "Do you need us to stay with you while she gets it fixed?"

"Naw," Laurel stopped her grooming to add to the story. "Mom is on the way. I have a cell phone if we need anything."

"A cell phone? At your age?" Sara laughed, and at that moment the kids abandoned us and ran to an attractive woman in her thirties who rushed through the automatic ER doors.

"Mommy, mommy," the kids shouted. The woman bent down and hugged the children, then quickly raced over to grandma.

"Uh, Mrs. Jaynes. We're ready in the back for you and Luke," a nurse attendant called out. She motioned for us to follow her into a room full of flimsy beds and gurneys, some of them hidden by curtains.

We saw three patients with broken bones, and a woman who had been bitten by a black widow spider. But, my thoughts kept returning to that older woman, Julia. I just couldn't understand why she didn't want to see me. Especially when everyone else seemed delighted to play with me.

It was getting late. Sara excused us and headed for the outer emergency department exit. She stopped and let go of my leash to dig out her keys from her purse. I looked back down the connecting hall to what I thought was the main part of the hospital. *Hmmn!* I thought. *Maybe I could just sneak back inside for a few minutes and find out what the deal was with that lady.*

Backing up, I turned and trotted down the hall. Through my fuzzy haze, I discovered what appeared to be a bank of elevators. They reminded me of the ones in the UCLA Medical Center when we went to find Sara. Soon, I was in full gallop, dragging my leash behind me.

By the time Sara realized that I'd taken off, I was already halfway across the room. "Luke, come on. We need to get home," she called out to me. "I have to make dinner. Where are you going?" Sara wasn't running, but she had begun to walk in my direction.

I paused for a moment and turned around in the direction of Sara's voice. Then, I turned back to look at the shinny metal elevator doors, then back to Sara.

"What is it? What do you want?" Sara had nearly caught up to me and was shrugging her shoulders in confusion.

A loud ding rung out and a green light shaped like an arrow lit up above the elevator. A set of double doors magically opened by themselves. The compartment appeared empty, so I stepped inside. Sara followed. I couldn't remember the floor Julia was on, so I looked at Sara and whimpered.

"What is it? Do you want more peanut butter? Is that it?" She looked at me with her palms upward to question me.

I barked because I knew that I was headed in the right direction. Or, at least I thought I was.

Sara joined me in the elevator, and the doors shut and up we went one floor. When the door opened, a number of people got on with us. Sara bent down and whispered, "Is this where you want to go?"

I didn't move a muscle. An older bald-headed man pushed the button for the fifth floor. When the doors opened, everyone got off. I took a whiff of the air and knew I'd found the place. With a muffled "ruff," I stepped off the elevator. Sara followed reluctantly.

I trotted down the hall toward what I thought was Julia's room.

"Luke, wait! Where are you going?" Sara tried to catch up with me.

I stopped short of the room and glanced up at the patient name plate on the wall. It looked fuzzy, but Sara would know if it was right.

"Oh, so that's it." Sara knelt next to me. "You want to see the patient that wouldn't let you visit last week. Well, I gotta warn you. She may not let us in again. We'll try. Wait here."

Sara stuck her head around the corner. I sat panting by the doorway.

"Hello, Julia. My name is Sara Jaynes. My therapy dog, Luke, and I tried to see you last week."

A labored voice struggled to answer. It was full of kindness and apology today, though. "Yes, I remember. I'm sorry. I didn't mean to be rude. It's just… well, I'm blind. Can't really see him, you know?"

"Oh, I'm so sorry. I didn't know. The nurse didn't tell us."

"That's all right," the older woman answered. "It's not like that's one of my best features, or anything." She laughed as the words left her lips.

"Well, Ms. Julia, I should tell you that you and my dog, Luke, have something in common. He's losing his eye sight and learning to feel his way around strange places and cope with it all."

"Really? A blind dog? Poor thing." She was quiet for a moment, then sat up in her chair. "Please, can you bring him to me? I'd like to touch him."

Sara picked up my leash and brought me into the room. "C'mon, boy. You got your wish."

As soon as I reached the side of Julia's wheelchair, she began to feel my face, then ran her hands the entire length of my body. "Arthur was my dog. He was so soft and furry. Lived to be about twelve, or so. Such a loyal soul. I miss him. It hurts to remember him now."

"I understand how you feel, Julia. Luke is such an important part of my world. Don't know what I'd do without him," Sara sat on a stool close to Julia's wheelchair.

"Oh, my, Sara, he's such a big, beautiful dog." Julia immediately embraced my large head and began to cry. I could feel her tears on my head. Carefully, I placed one paw and then the other on the side of her armrest and lifted my front legs to hover

over her lap. Her tears became laughter, and she began to talk to me.

"What a funny boy you are! I love Luke's personality. Tell me about him, Sara."

Sara chuckled. "Well, he's four years old. He was a birthday present for my husband, Ash. He's the smartest dog I've ever known. He even led me back to you just now if you can believe it. I think he really wanted to meet you."

"Is that right? Well, Luke, I'm mighty proud to meet you." Julia started scratching me behind my ears. She picked the perfect spot.

"I'm sorry to cut this short, Julia. The thing is, we were just about out the door when Luke decided to come back up and see you. We really need to get home now, but we'd love to see you again sometime soon. May we come back and visit you next week?"

Julia sighed. The scratching behind my ears abruptly ceased. I took that as my cue to return my front paws to the floor.

"I'll be upset if you don't, Sara. Goodbye, Luke. See you soon, even if I can't really see."

I decided to give her a proper goodbye. I leaped back up with my front paws on her armrests. Then, I gave her face a good washing. I think she had been eating apple sauce before we got there, because I could still taste it off her cheeks.

Julia began to laugh. "Whoa... he he, okay, thanks, Luke. That'll do." She laughed some more. "My, I haven't giggled like that in what seems like years!"

"I'm sorry, Julia. Luke shouldn't have been so aggressive with you." Sara touched the woman's hand. Are you all right?"

"No, no, Sara. I loved every second of it, and I'm fine." Julia waved goodbye.

As we left, I somehow knew that Julia was going to be important to me. I think Sara sensed it as well. This would be the first of many visits to come.

****

Sara drove us home quickly with no stops. We went immediately into the kitchen to prepare dinner. "Hey, Ash," she called out. "We're home. In the kitchen."

"Be there in a sec," he yelled back from his office.

Sara quickly fixed my kibble, mixing it with some grated cheese and chopped chicken. I gobbled it down while she rattled the pots and pans. She seemed frustrated.

"What's all the noise in here?" Ashlundt sauntered in. "What're we having?"

"Pasta with Pesto, salad, garlic bread," She shouted back. All this shouting over the bubbling water and sizzling frying pan was hurting my ears.

"Sounds good."

"Yeah, I'm running late. Got held up at the hospital."

"Hey, babe, there's no rush. Slow down." He patted his stomach. "I might need to work out after all those carbs."

I barked aloud once, volunteering to help with the workout if it meant us going for a long walk.

Ashlundt bent down and patted me on the back. Then, he looked back at Sara, flashing a puzzled expression. "Oh, by the way, I've been trying to get hold of Luke's breeder, but I just get voice mail. Been trying to call him for weeks."

"Why?" She stopped in mid stir and looked at him. "What's the deal?"

"Well, I wanna find out the background on Luke's parents. See what caused his loss of eyesight. You know, make sure that everything is on the up-and-up." He patted my head lightly once again.

Sara stopped and turned to him. "But why, Ash? It won't change anything."

"No, but I want to talk to him. Got a lot of questions for him. It won't bring back Luke's sight, but it might give me some satisfaction."

"Ash, I hope you aren't going to beat the man up over the phone about this." Sara's face appeared a bit twisted in worry.

Ashlundt scratched his head. "Well, no. Not beat him up. I just want to know who's responsible."

"But you aren't. Isn't that all that matters? Look, Ash, it would be more of a help to me if you *participated* a little more with helping Luke get ready for the lights to go out. Is that too much to ask? Priorities, you know?" She turned back to the stove.

He moved closer to her. "No, no. Look, I understand. It's just… I've just been really busy, Sara. You said you'd handle the therapy dog thing. And I'm sure you're doing a great job with it."

Sara dropped the wooden spoon on the counter and turned to face Ashlundt. "I don't think you get it. That's not what I mean. I wanted to talk to you about this over dinner."

Ashlundt shrugged his shoulders. "Then what do you mean?"

"You really don't get it, do you?" Sara was sounding upset. "You think this is about the volunteer work? Are you serious? No, you really don't have a clue, do you?"

Ashlundt stood silent for about a minute, staring down at the floor. I could smell his anger coming to a boil, but I also sensed that he was trying to contain it. He let out a deep sigh. "Okay, Sara. Fine. I guess I don't get it. I thought I was helping with my best effort. But if that's not good enough…" He stomped out of the kitchen and headed back into his office, calling over his shoulder, "Just call me when dinner's ready."

They ate in silence that night. Sara didn't discuss what had been on her mind, and I realized that I had witnessed their first argument since their wedding.

****

Sara and I asked to visit Julia the following week. We had a promise to keep.

"She's not doing very well today, Sara." The nurse on duty Sara called Caroline gave me a nice teaspoon of peanut butter. "She had a rough night. Did you know that she's in her nineties?"

Sara moved closer to Caroline as if to whisper a secret. "You're kidding. She doesn't look that old. Wrinkled yes, but that hair; it's so white and curly. And she has impressive bone structure, don't you think?"

"Yes, she's amazing," Caroline agreed. "But she's in congestive heart failure. Even the slightest exertion is exhausting for her. Keep that in mind when you're with her. Keep your visit short today."

"Is she… dying?" Sara ventured this question with trepidation in her voice.

"It's not great. At the rate she's going, it won't be very long. A month or two at the most. But, you never know."

My heart leaped in my chest. It hurt to hear that I might lose this new friend so quickly. I hoped that the nurse's prediction was wrong.

Sara led me to Julia's room. "Hi, Julia. It's Luke and Sara. We've come by to see how you're doing." Sara held me back, probably so that I wouldn't jump into bed with Julia and startle her after the instructions that Caroline had just given.

Julia's voice was even more shaky. "Good morning, Sa-Sara. Hello, Luke. Come in you two. Tell me all about your week. Sor - Sorry I'm not up in my chair."

Sara glanced around the small room. She spotted a chair in the corner and pulled it next to the bed. I hopped up to the bed level, leaned in slowly, then covered Julia's fragile face with gentle kisses.

"I'm so glad you could make it." Julia patted her hand on her bed, gesturing for me to come up on the bed with her.

I wanted to climb right in and snuggle with her, but I knew the drill. I waited for Sara to find a white sheet in the closet and spread it down on the bed. Next, Sara guided me up to the bed and gently took Julia's hand to let her know that we were alongside her. I felt Julia's entire body relax with the comfort I brought her. Her voice became steadier.

"So, Luke," Julia began, "Are you finding your way around pretty well?" She moved her jittery hands across my back until she found my face. "Well, let me tell you, dear boy, about the good and the bad of losing your sight."

I gave a soft, muffled bark to acknowledge that Julia was speaking to me. I then leaned forward and licked what tasted like vanilla pudding off the corner of her mouth.

Julia giggled. "Luke, my friend, you will miss the loss of the faces that you love the most. You'll regret not being able to see the beauty of a summer day, or the trees as they sway in the breeze, or watching children playing." She squirmed a bit, attempting to sit upright in the bed. "But you will gain so many delightful things. I can only imagine how well you can smell, but your ability... it will be so intensified. Sounds will be so crystal clear to you. You'll notice every sound, all at once. The pleasure of a warm touch is exquisite, my furry one. You'll revel in all the things we take for granted when we can see." She sighed as she stroked my head.

I laid my face against her thin shoulder and exhaled heavily. The way Julia described blindness, it didn't really sound so terrible at all. It sounded more like a new adventure. A whole new way of seeing the world, only without sight to guide me. I was so grateful to Julia for knowing what to expect.

Sara and I became frequent visitors to Julia, often going to see only her several times a week. Each time, she would warm my heart by sharing her life with me.

"I wasn't always blind, you know. I was an aviator back in the forties. Pretty rare for women to fly planes back then. My husband, he was a pilot during the Second World War. Afterward, he taught me to fly. We had our own crop dusting company in the San Joaquin Valley. Did really well."

I licked her hand to encourage her storytelling.

"Then I got glaucoma. That was the end of my flying days." Julia sighed deeply. "But I'll never forget what I had seen. Can you imagine how beautiful the earth and the sky are at 20,000 feet?"

I snuggled a little closer to her and tried to grasp what she was describing. I didn't understand 20,000 feet. I'd never flown in an airplane, but I did often look up to the sky and wonder what the world looked like from the clouds.

Sara ran her pinky across Julia's arm. "Maybe you'd better describe it for us."

"Sure. I'd love to. Well, the earth, it looks like a map. All the rock formations, crops, housing developments – everything has a distinct design. All the colors are greens and browns. Water is blue, of course. And the sky! Well, the clouds are like fluffy cotton balls against the pure blue. Now, Luke, all you have to do is smell the salty air of the ocean and the peaty earthiness of the soil. Think about how the grass smells after rain, or how the breeze caresses your face. And then you'll always remember how those things looked."

I closed my eyes and tried to imagine. I thought about the sky and the clouds. And the wind as it made the trees sway. My time with Julia gave me an enthusiasm for the sighted world and all that I would miss as I struggled with a blurry world. But she told it to me in a way that would help me replace the loss of seeing it. This was one of the greatest gifts I ever received.

****

I had thought that Ashlundt would be more involved. He sounded so positive on that day back at the vet's office. He was still kind and loving to me, but he didn't seem to be with us as much as he had been before my diagnosis.

Sara's frustration with him seemed to be growing. After we returned home from a great visit with Julia one late afternoon, she sought out Ashlundt in his office. I followed and stood next to her in the doorway.

"Sara, hi. I'm glad you're home. I spoke to George Brown." He stopped typing on his keyboard.

"Yes, I see that a few more books have been added to your collection on the floor, Ash." Sara's voice held a hint of sarcasm.

"Yeah. I finally got to ask him how this could have happened. You know, the hereditary blindness."

"Did you accuse the poor man of something, Ash?" Sara was leaning forward in the doorway, and I wandered over to my office bed.

"No, I told him that my perfect puppy was going blind from some degenerative disease, and that I thought he'd sold us a healthy dog!" He was rocking back and forth in his desk chair, making creaking sounds as he moved. It was making me nervous.

"Oh, Ash. Why blame him? He can't change it." Sara entered the room and began to pace as she spoke to him. "And it's not like we're going to exchange Luke for another dog, get our money back!"

He stopped rocking and stared at her. "Well, he told me that Luke was sired from Chester of Leicester, a champion from England, which we already knew. The mother was out of another champion line. Something else he told us back then. He said he had no knowledge of any wrong doing."

"There you go. It wasn't his fault, Ash." Sara stopped in front of him, her hands palms up from what I could tell.

"No, there's more. He admitted that after he sold us Luke and the rest of the litter, he found out he'd been duped."

"How?" Sara put her hand on his shoulder.

I waited with anticipation on my bed for his next words.

"I asked him what he meant and why he didn't bother telling us about it until now." He took her hand from his shoulder and held it. "I mean, maybe we could have done something to prevent it."

"Ash, you know as well as I do that there's nothing to do about a genetic defect after-the-fact."

He ignored her comment, released her hand and continued reporting back the conversation. "Then, he confessed that some of Luke's littermates started going blind as early as when they were a year old! He did some investigating and found out that the sire was a carrier. He said we couldn't blame him for this and that he'd done nothing wrong."

Sara plopped down on a stool next to his desk. "But, Ash, I'm not surprised. That's the way a defect like this would come down. Let's just move on."

"Move on? Sara, my God! The entire litter has this thing! They are either blind or carriers." Ashlundt lurched forward in his chair. His sudden movement startled me. "All those poor sweet puppies. It's heartbreaking."

"Yes. It is. And it's hard for us and for Luke. But again, what do you expect the breeder to do about it now?" She seemed to stare up at him intently.

"Well, actually, he said he neutered the sire so he couldn't pass it on. Then, he wanted to know if Luke was neutered. I told him he was."

"And?"

"I asked him how he couldn't know about this." He leaned closer to her. "I mean, Sara, I know you researched the guy, didn't you? Isn't he supposed to be the most reputable Lab breeder in this area?"

Sara jumped up from the stool as if attacked. "Yes, Ash! I did my research! He's been in business for forty years."

"Calm down. I'm not saying you did anything wrong." Ashlundt's voice grew defensive. "He offered to refund the money you paid for Luke. He even offered to pay us $1,200."

"I hope you didn't take him up on it, Ash." She put her arm out in a gesture as if to stop him from doing something.

"No." Ashlundt seemed to become less agitated. "I told him I knew he didn't do this on purpose. I imagine it's hurt his business enough. But... maybe he shouldn't be in business anyway."

"Did you say that, Ash? How could you? Think about what you went through after the lawsuit." Sara's tone was scolding.

"No, I didn't say he shouldn't be in business. He said he was still trying to recover from it. He said he worked years to build up a top reputation, then this one little incident nearly wiped him out. I can relate to that." Ashlundt wiped at his eyes as if to clear them.

"I hope you told him that, Ash." Sara reached over and pushed a blonde lock from his forehead.

"No… I didn't. I told him that was punishment enough." Ashlundt shrugged. "Our poor Luke… it's really so hard to watch him struggle like this."

Sara stood in silence starring at Ashlundt. Finally, she put her hands on her hips and released her disgust. "How could you not empathize with that poor man? Have you no compassion for what he's been through? You're a psychologist, for God's sake! Why do you think he couldn't have been duped! You, of all people! How would you feel if your patients said those things to you?"

He stood up, shaking. "Well, some of them did!"

"And that justifies it, Ash? *That* justifies not helping more with Luke? I'm ashamed of you." Sara turned on her heels and stomped out of the office.

I quivered in my doggie bed in the corner. Sara was upset. I wondered if she was frustrated because Ashlundt hadn't forgiven my breeder or if something deeper could be bothering her.

Ashlundt sat back down in his office chair, then swiveled around and stared at me. He looked like he was shaking his head. I couldn't tell for sure, but it almost seemed like he was angry with me. Without a word, he got up and knelt down next to me. I wagged my tail so hard it thumped on my dog bed. He looked me in the eyes and sighed, "Oh, Luke. What a storm we've gotten ourselves into." Without another word, he stood back up and headed across the hall to the garage. I heard the car drive off moments later.

****

Sara and I went back to Northridge Hospital to see Julia later that week. A nurse had called Sara that morning to tell us that Julia had grown weaker over the past few days. Her wheelchair was nowhere to be found. Perhaps someone else was using it. Julia was in bed again when we arrived.

The moment I entered her room, I could smell it… death. I stopped in the doorway. It startled me. And the smell frightened me. I knew it would be the last time that I would be with Julia. She was so weak that she could barely put her arms around me.

Sara positioned me on the bed next to her, so I could just be close to her.

Julia's breathing was labored. She struggled with her words. "Luke… my friend. Sara… sweet girl. Looks like… this is… it."

She knows I thought to myself. The sadness of it all left a lump in my throat.

"Don't try to talk, Julia. Just let us sit here with you for a while." Sara stroked Julia's forehead gently.

"No… want to tell you. Thank you for the… joy you have brought me these last… weeks.

"No, thank you, Julia. You've given Luke and me so much insight. You mean so much to him, and to me." Sara squeezed Julia's thin shoulder then sat in a chair next to the bed.

Julia was quiet, almost dozing for a long while. I lay still with my head next to hers. Her heartbeat sounded slower than I remembered.

One of the nurses came to the bedside and took Julia's pulse and checked a machine they called a heart monitor now attached to her. "She's very weak, Sara. You should probably say your goodbyes now. The family's on the way to be with her."

Julia awoke to the nurse's voice. "No, wait. Let me. Let me say goodbye to Luke." She seemed to have sudden clarity. She found my head with her hands. "Goodbye, my friend. I hope that humans are allowed at the Rainbow Bridge. I'll wait for you there."

"The Rainbow Bridge, Julia?" Sara was confused.

"You know." Julia made a circular motion upward with her right hand. "Where animals go to heaven."

Sara let out a sob and reached over to gently hug Julia. "Goodbye, Julia. It's been such a joy to know you."

One last time I covered Julia's face and hands with kisses and licked the tears from her eyes. Sara helped me down from the bed and walked me to the door. We both turned back toward her bed. In that moment, the light streamed through the window, and I could see her beautiful old face framed by white silvery hair. My heart ached to know that this was our last time together. I knew I would never forget her. I hoped there was a Rainbow Bridge – whatever that was – and that she would be there for me someday.

Julia was a gift that Sara gave to me. Yet, I also felt Sara and I had been guided to Julia as if we were destined to meet, however briefly. Julia had helped me accept my impending blindness. Sara and Julia allowed me so much comfort through this process. Their love for me was without rules or expectations.

Chapter Nine

The Darkness

Their son Colson was crawling and starting to stand up when the last rays of light fell dark on my eyes. I could no longer see anything at night, but I had become quite adept at navigating around the yard and on the street with Sara on our twilight walks. Sara had become my primary caregiver, and even though I still sat with Ashlundt in his office, his "chats" with me had diminished. It was depressing.

It all seemed logical. He was busy with his work and taking care of the baby. But, all the attention heaped on Colson made me more than a little jealous at first.

I sat listening to Ashlundt in his office on the phone one afternoon. His irritability had been growing throughout the day.

"I don't care if the association conference call was postponed, Eric. Why didn't I get an email about it?" He hit the disconnect button on his phone and picked up a three-ring binder and threw it across the room. Another human temper tantrum. I was getting so used to the thud of books hitting his floor that I just tuned it out most of the time.

I stood up, walked over to him and put my head on his knee, wagging my tail.

He rubbed my head, and I felt the tension in his hand. "Not now, Lukey."

I wondered what was bothering him so much. He seemed full of frustration. I slunk over to the doorway, sat back on my haunches and waited.

Ashlundt's temper seemed to calm again as he made another phone call. But after he hung up, he jumped up and pushed past me. *Why did he not pay more attention to me? He wasn't unkind; he just didn't take the time to be with me as he had before.* He'd delegated my feedings to Sara and no longer walked with us even when he had time, but rather opted to play with Colson. *I loved him and missed his companionship.* The sadness from his absence covered me like a cold blanket that I couldn't shake off. *Did he think his behavior would protect him from some future hurt that my blindness might cause him? Had he not learned a valuable lesson when he almost lost Sara?*

He even inadvertently shut me out of the joy of Sara's pregnancy. The day that Sara confirmed her pregnancy with her doctor, she took me quietly into the master bathroom. This was the area of our home that I considered the "crying room" because it was where we had always dealt with her fear of cancer. I dreaded she had something bad to tell me. She either cried or agonized in that bathroom. Instead, she dropped to her knees and hugged me. "Oh, Lukey, I'm so happy! I'm gonna have a baby. Just think; a little one that can be your best friend. I haven't told Ash yet. I can't wait to see his face." She was so full of happiness, and I licked her face and hands trying to convey my excitement for her, for all of us.

That evening, she set the little-used dining room next to the kitchen to a celebratory atmosphere. There were candles lit on the table, a beautiful silk tablecloth – Sara said it was red. She put out the best wedding gift china along with crystal champagne flutes at each setting. That night over dinner, she poured Ashlundt a glass of Dom Pérignon and sat next to him.

"Wow, Sara. This is really nice. What's the occasion?" He raised his glass to toast. "Hey, aren't you going to have any champagne, my love?" His affection toward Sara was strong.

"Nope. It wouldn't be very good for us right now."

"Us? What do you mean?" He stared at her expectantly.

"I mean, champagne wouldn't be good for the baby." I could hear the excited tremble in her voice.

I tried as hard as I could to see the look on Ashlundt's face, but he jumped up suddenly and whirled Sara around the room, all the while shouting, "A baby! We're having a baby!"

I ran to his side and barked my happiness, but he was too busy carrying Sara through the kitchen into the adjoining den. He placed her gently on the sofa, then sat down beside her and pulled her on his lap. He was as giddy as I'd ever seen him.

"Hey, maybe it's time we start planning on converting one of the guest rooms for the baby. Maybe it will be a boy, Sara. Wouldn't it be wonderful if we had a son? I could teach him how to surf, how to play ball." I heard him jump up quickly, then sit down. He was almost unable to contain himself.

"A girl can do those things too, you know, Mr. Man," Sara teased. I focused intently on them and saw her poke him in the chest and tickle him. His laughter filled the house.

I gave them some time together as he held her, kissed her and told her that he loved her and was so grateful to her for this wonderful gift. "I don't care if it's a boy or girl – just a baby!" he announced. Then, I slowly crawled up on the sofa toward them. Sara quickly reached out to hug me. Ashlundt gave me a quick pat on the head. It ended too quickly. Ashlundt picked Sara up and walked away with her to the kitchen. I don't think he meant to exclude me; he was just carried away. But, I had never before felt so conflicted by joy and sheer abandonment.

****

"We're gonna throw Sara a baby shower," Corky announced in our backyard. "It'll be your first, so you might as well collect on all those baby things that you don't have in the house. You know, blankets, a playpen, the diaper genie."

"Oh, it sounds great!" Sara hugged herself. "I've been to so many of those at work, and even at school. But I never thought I'd be having one for me."

Corky laughed. "Well, honey, it's your time. So we gotta do it right. I'm gonna invite all the neighbors, your friends from school and work. Everyone."

I gave out a bark of excitement. Corky must have thought I was seeking attention.

"Oh, and we can have Luke there too, of course. We'll let him roll around in all the wrapping paper and empty boxes. He'll love that." I felt Corky's plump hand on my head.

"Uh, actually Corky, that's a bad idea." Ashlundt chimed in." It'll be too crowded for him. Now that he's almost blind, he'd probably bump into people. We wouldn't want him to get hurt in the crowd."

Sara threw her hands up in protest from what I could tell. "Ash, no. Luke's part of our family. Everyone loves him. He won't be in the way."

Corky also tried to intercede on my behalf. "Ash, Luke is always welcome at my house, and he really doesn't bump into anything. We even used my house as a training ground for his blindness." She leaned toward him with one elbow on her Capri-clad knee. "He knows the terrain."

Ashlundt was adamant. "Look, girls. I know you think it'll be easy for Luke to thread through a bunch of people at a party, but it won't be." He stood up and walked around the back of Sara's chair. "He doesn't have to go everywhere with us. I'm sure he'll be okay with it." He returned to his chair across from the two women.

"Since when?" Sara leaned forward and looked him in the eye, or at least that seemed like what she was doing.

"Look, honey. Taking Luke to navigate through a room full of people is unfair to him. He could get his tail stepped on. He might step on something sharp." He leaned back and crossed his legs. "Who knows what?"

"Ash. I don't know a single friend of either of you who doesn't adore Luke. He'll be fine. Why wouldn't he?" Corky seemed puzzled.

"But he's going to have limitations from now on. It's just easier not to have to worry about him stumbling around at a party." Ashlundt threw up his hands in annoyance. "We just need to be more protective, that's all."

Sara stood up from her patio chair, hands on hips, "Whatever! Come on, Corky; let's take Luke for a walk. If he can manage walking trails, he sure as hell can manage a party!"

****

I stayed home the day of the baby shower, listening to the sounds of laughter and the smell of Corky's incredible freshly baked pumpkin bread wafting across the street. I'd never felt so left out of anything. Sara brought me a plate full of Corky's delicious sausage balls as consolation. I knew that she loved me, that I would always be her dear friend. But after Colson was born,

Ashlundt's attention shifted even more away from me and toward his son. This was more devastating than the loss of my eyesight.

****

The morning that it happened, I woke early as usual and went into Colson's room. I could hear him laughing as Sara readied him for the day. She placed him on a blanket on the floor where I could smell him and he could squeal and roll over on me. It was our daily habit. Even though Colson was Ashlundt's focal point, my love for the little one never wavered.

Sara wanted us to be close friends, which we had become. Colson was beautiful with his daddy's light hair and his mother's dark eyes, or so everyone said. Corky told me that Colson had Sara's smattering of freckles across the bridge of his nose. I could almost picture it in my mind. And Colson always smelled of baby powder and goodness.

I knew it wouldn't be long now, so I memorized his face so that I could keep it with me always. I crawled as close to his nose as I could get and watched as the droplets of drool fell from his chin. He was teething, and two small bottom teeth were prominent when he smiled. It was a wide smile, and he always had one ready whenever he looked at me. I knew even then that the boy, like his mother, returned my love completely. He didn't care if I was blind or whole. He pulled my ears, slobbered on my face and shared his toys with me. We rolled around on the blanket in our morning ritual.

We were steadfast friends. Sara always trusted me to watch him or play with him when she ran to throw a load of laundry in, or fix something in the kitchen. I was always by her side while she cared for him, and I stayed close to him whenever she had to go out and leave him with a babysitter. I felt it was my job to look after him when she was gone.

We continued to play on the blanket. He offered me one of his teething rings, but before I could take it, Ashlundt suddenly entered the room, scooped the boy up and raised him high above his head. "That's my boy; you're the best; yes, you are!"

Colson squealed when Ashlundt buried his face in the boy's bare stomach and made motor boat sounds. I couldn't stop wagging my tail at the joy of it all. Ashlundt tucked the boy under his arm and strode off to fix his breakfast without even a glance in my direction. My happy barking turned into whines of rejection.

Sara bent down and gave me a warm hug. "It's all right, Lukey. Ash still loves you. He's just absorbed with Colson right now."

She sat for a long time next to me. Her warmth became my sustenance while I stared out the window of the nursery and watched the morning sun slowly fade to darkness. I was glad Colson's was the last face I ever saw.

****

I became a master over the darkness. I could navigate my way through the house with expert ease. When we left our neighborhood, I learned to carefully place my front paws ahead of me and cautiously follow Sara's scent of flowers. Throughout her pregnancy, and even after Colson was born, Sara and I continued our therapy dog sessions at hospitals on Thursday afternoons. I became particularly popular with patients and hospital staff after I went completely blind. Everyone was amazed to see the blind dog stick to her like Velcro.

It became habit for us to take Friday afternoons off from work and go to the West Hills Park to play. Sometimes we'd alternate and go to a dog park so that Colson and I could both play with other dogs. Ashlundt always joined in – anything for Colson. The boy ran everywhere by then, and he loved nothing better than the park.

We planned to go to the West Hills Park one Friday afternoon. By that time, I had been blind for what seemed a long time. That day, Sara even packed a picnic lunch. I sat in the kitchen, and she described the picnic to me: "PBJ for Colson; turkey on whole wheat for Ash and me; chips, grapes, chocolate chip cookies and special pepperoni treats for Luke."

Of course I knew I'd get half of Colson's PBJ, chips and cookies. He always shared.

While they loaded the SUV, Ashlundt's cell phone rang.

My senses now heightened, I listened to his words.

"Dr. Jaynes speaking… Stay calm and tell me the problem, Howard… Yes, yes, I understand. No, it's not a problem. I can be there in 20 minutes."

I heard him disconnect the call, then step toward Sara. "I'm so sorry. That's one of my patients. He's having a meltdown. Will you be okay at the park alone today?"

"Of course, silly. Go to your patient. We'll be just fine."

I thought about it for a minute. I was hoping that this meant that we could go to the dog park instead. The regular park was near a busy street. The dog park was completely fenced. I'd need to stay alert to make sure everyone stayed safe without Ashlundt there. This wasn't going to be easy.

It became a fleeting thought once I was in the backseat in the SUV leaning next to Colson in his car seat. He kept feeding me his cheesy goldfish crackers. I was in heaven. The park, Sara and Colson, snacks… what could be better?

Soon, a full belly of pepperoni and half of Colson's lunch made me sleepy in the sunshine of the late afternoon. The feel of the fleece blanket on my nose, and the warmth of Colson pressed up to me… it was pure bliss. After lunch, Colson and I had played with the jingle ball Sara kept in stock for me. I could play ball as long as it had a bell inside it so I could follow the sound. Unfortunately, the sound of the bells tied to Colson's shoes and the ones in the ball confused me at times. But I usually found the ball, often knocking the boy down in a heap of laughter as I skirted to fetch for him. I could feel Sara's presence making sure we didn't get too close to the street. Now, we stretched out together, tired from our play.

The ring of Sara's cell phone aroused me. I could hear her voice answering and then fading a bit as if she was walking away to not disturb us. I felt Colson stir next to me, then shift away. I snuggled back down to drift off when I heard the jingling of his shoe bells and jumped up to follow. He was running fast and laughing and throwing the ball again. I was frantic to catch him. I ran hard and finally overtook him to knock him down on the soft grass. He squealed with laughter and threw the ball again, this time in the same direction that he was running. Suddenly, I felt the grassy footing change to sidewalk pavement. Something wasn't right. I began to bark hysterically. I heard Sara's voice in the distance.

"Colson, No! Stop! Colson, Colson! Oh my God!"

Her voice was cut off by the screeching of car breaks and the little one's shrill scream. It was the most terrifying sound I'd ever heard in my life.

I felt my way to the curb and stepped into the street, letting the smell of blood draw me to the child's limp body. I began to lick his wounds frantically only to be pulled back by the collar and Sara's sharp hysterical command. "Luke! Stay!"

Her screams of agony broke into sobs and a man's voice. "Oh, my God, lady. He just darted out between the parked cars! He was so quick! I… I couldn't get out of his way!"

Another frantic voice screamed, "Call 911!"

The voices around me faded as the shock of it all set in. Our world had changed forever, and all I could do was sit in darkness and fear and wait for the confirmation of what I knew had happened.

****

I sat outside the Emergency Room where Colson had been brought. My heart was broken. I knew that my little friend was gone forever. I smelled his death upon him as they loaded him into the ambulance.

I prayed that Ashlundt wouldn't blame Sara or me for Colson's accident. I hoped if he was angry that it would be directed at me. Sara had lost her only child. What she needed at that moment was consolation and sympathy from her husband. *That was what he must give her.*

Humans too often spent time attaching responsibility or blame to others. I had seen Ashlundt try to do that with my breeder. But what they should do is offer each other support. Forgiving someone we love should be the easiest thing in the world to do. Shouldn't it? Ashlundt couldn't blame us. He wouldn't multiply the pain and suffering by holding back his forgiveness for Colson's loss. I thought about how things would actually not be so difficult for humans if only they would remove their unwillingness to forgive, along with their selfishness and fears.

I sat for a very long time next to the door. I smelled Ashlundt's familiar scent of bay leaf and ocean when he passed through the ER door. I waited even longer. People came up to me and petted me. One nurse offered me a bowl of water. I remained aloof, not wanting to be distracted in case Sara came for me. It was long past my evening meal when I heard them come outside to me. I heard nothing except Sara's voice, full of despair. "Come, Luke." She took me by the collar and led me to the car.

They rode in silence. I sat in the back, leaning on Colson's empty car seat, wishing I could have done something, anything to have prevented this horrific accident. Once the car stopped, I heard the passenger door open, then the backseat door. Sara whispered, "Come, Luke." I obeyed. I heard the car back out of the driveway and leave. Slowly, I followed Sara into the house.

She said nothing as she fixed my meal and left the room. I realized that the scene I hoped for at the hospital had not occurred. It seemed apparent that it had been just the opposite. After sating my hunger, I went to find Sara in her bedroom. She lay across her bed in silence, tortured and bereft. Even though I wasn't usually allowed on the bed, she said nothing when I crawled up next to her and placed my head on her hip. I gave out a whimpered cry of sorrow.

Carol McKibben

Chapter Ten

The Punishment

We laid together in silence for a long, long time. I had to go outside so badly that my bladder hurt, but I didn't dare leave Sara. She was so cold. I wanted her to feel my warmth, the warmth that Ashlundt should have offered. Soon, my stomach began to growl and added to my discomfort, but it didn't matter. I would not leave her until he came back. It must have been morning because the phone started ringing. All those distraught voices leaving messages of sorrow on our answering machine. Tim and Corky, then Dr. Wild. I didn't know how they knew about Colson. They just did. Still, Sara didn't move. I crawled up to her face, pressing my nose on her cheek to see if she was asleep. Her hand softly touched the top of my head. "It's okay, Lukey. Thank you for staying with me." A ragged sigh escaped from her and was joined by my own.

As we lay there, my mind drifted to Colson in happier times. I fell in love with him the day they brought him home from the hospital. I was so focused on protecting the new baby that it made Ashlundt nervous. He kept hovering over his son and repeating: "Sara, please keep an eye on Luke; he seems a little obsessed."

"Ash, take a chill pill," Sara would laugh. "Luke would never hurt anyone, much less Colson. He's just curious and infatuated with our beautiful son... like we are."

She was right. Colson, even as an infant, had a charisma about him. I was drawn to him, wanted to be near him and protect him. His personality evolved into one of warmth, humor and intelligence. I knew that when he became an adult that he would be engaging, drawing others to him and ultimately being admired by men and women alike. Since his birth, Ashlundt's mother, Anya, and father, Asa, had made frequent visits, often staying with us for a week at a time. They were a witty couple who looked like throwbacks to what Sara called "the hippie era." Asa was tall like Ashlundt, still slender with long gray hair. His son had his identical steel blue eyes. Anya was like Mother Earth with her herbs and holistic medicine. She often went into our backyard and picked flowers to wind into her long sandy hair that she wove into a single braid. I heard her tell Asa that Colson's toddler face was taking on Ashlundt's strong nose and chin. She described his eyes as "gorgeous and full of Sara's compassion and goodness."

Our daily routine allowed me to be with Colson all the time, except when he slept. Even then, I would lay quietly in the nursery with him, sometimes napping myself. Sara took time off before and after Colson was born. Eventually, she went back to school and back to the clinic part-time. The many months of Sara's maternity break were a wonderful time for me. Colson and Sara became my world. I even learned how to fetch clean diapers and bottles whenever Sara needed them. When Colson grew older, I enjoyed all-the-more devouring the assorted scraps of food that he threw off his highchair tray. Cucumber slices, Cheerios, you name it.

His sudden loss left a hole in my heart that never healed. Just like humans, dogs mourn the loss of those they love. I thought of our friend, Julia, every day. I missed not being with her when we visited the hospital. I missed her stories and her tenderness. I missed Colson's unconditional friendship and love. I vowed to carry Colson's memory with me always. I tried to fill the hole in my heart with memories of both of them.

I was still curled up on the bed next to Sara when the familiar sound of jingling keys roused me. I popped my head up and listened closer. It was coming from outside of Ashlundt's patient entrance. The sound of a key being inserted into the lock had me sitting up. Soon Ashlundt's familiar footsteps walked toward us. His weight pushed down our side of the bed. Sara let out a lone sob.

"It's all right, Sara. I'm here." Ashlundt's voice was soothing.

I decided to give them a moment of privacy. That, and the fact that I needed to pee so terribly. I leaped off the bed, headed for the doggie door in the kitchen and raced out to the backyard. After a very large drink from my water dish back in the kitchen, I felt my way back to the bedroom, plopped down on my own bed and listened.

"Sara, I don't understand how this could have happened. I'm not thinking straight right now. I just want Colson back." I heard his muffled agony and knew he must have his face buried in her neck like I used to observe. At least he was finally there for her.

She said nothing but her tears became great gulping sobs as she cried out. "Colson, oh, my sweet baby. I couldn't stop… him… the street."

I felt miserably helpless. If I could have only *seen* him, watched over him, I might have saved him.

****

They buried him in the Chatsworth Park Cemetery not far from our house. It was one of those rare rainy days in Southern California. The weather fit the mood of all of our heavy hearts. Tim and Corky were staunch rocks for my humans. Tim even handled all the funeral arrangements since Ashlundt and Sara were too distraught to do it. Corky said she would make sure that the flowers were beautiful, and afterwards everyone was invited back to the Bensons' home.

Asa, Anya, and Ashlundt's siblings, Ardin and Asmara, all arrived two days before to help with anything they could. Asmara was the youngest brother and a senior at UC San Diego. Ardin, the eldest, was a cardio-vascular surgeon. Unfortunately, the three brothers were not particularly close. Asmara had always liked me, so we spent a lot of time hiking in the woods together. He was an environmental studies major and was more comfortable outdoors than anywhere. Ardin appeared to do a little too much big brothering for Ashlundt's liking, always making the decisions on what and where the family would eat, or how he thought his younger brother should handle his life and his business. "Why do you insist on a home office, Ash? You should have your own clinic," he would often urge.

Asa and Anya were typically laid back and just available to support wherever needed. But, they were all very helpful to Ashlundt and Sara, and their presence comforted the three of us.

Dr. Wild came by the house before the funeral and took me in her Jeep to the cemetery. Ashlundt didn't object to my presence. I kept a low profile and listened to conversations among all of the same friends and family who had attended the wedding.

"Son, your mother and I are here for you," Asa's voice shook with the words.

"I know, Dad." I could hear them patting each other on the back while Sara and Anya sobbed together.

"I can't believe this is happening!" Debi, Sara's best friend, sounded as if she was hugging both Sara and Anya.

I tried to focus on anything that would stop my heart from breaking. The smell of large varieties of flowers filled the air. Then, Suzi Wild took my collar and led me next to Sara, placing me in between the two of them for the graveside service. As Colson's small coffin was lowered into its grave, my beloved Sara dropped to her knees and buried her head in my neck. I let out a yelp of despair. Sara's tears mingled with the rain on my neck. I heard Ashlundt let out a huge wrenching sob and drop to the ground next to her. The hole in my heart became even wider. It was the absolute darkest moment of my life.

****

Ashlundt became driven again after losing Colson. He plunged into building up his practice. Following the advice of his brother, Ardin, he took on an associate psychologist. Next, he opened a "real" office outside of the house. He spent most of his time buried in his work, leaving us alone with our sadness in our all-too-empty home. Sara turned to me for her primary companionship.

We took long meandering walks in the nearby woods. It was the same every day. All I could hear were the chirping of the birds, the crackle of the twigs under Sara's feet and her quiet sobs.

"Oh, Luke. If only I'd not taken the phone call. If I hadn't walked away from the blanket... he might be with us now..." We'd stop while she sat on a rotting log, crying even harder.

"It's so hard to hold it all... together in front of others. You're the only one... the only one who understands." She would always wrap her arms around me and hold me close.

Her pain was heavy, as was the air that surrounded us. All I could do was lay my head in her lap and let her sob it out. I wished that the tears would carry away her pain and melt into me. I wished that all the pain could somehow be transferred into my body so that Sara would finally feel somewhat better.

One afternoon, when we weren't in the woods, Corky knocked on our front door, and I felt my way over to it. Sara let her inside. Corky patted me on the head lovingly. "Sara, I've been calling and calling, leaving you messages. You need to get out. You and Ash, come to dinner with Tim and me."

"I'm not ready for that yet, Corky. But thanks." I heard her stifle a sob.

"Sara, it's been months. At least come to our house for dinner." Corky's voice was pleading now.

"Corky, please. I can't. Not now." Sara was adamant, so Corky quietly hugged her and, knowing it was useless, slipped out the door.

More solitude. It seemed we were destined for it. I too was still grieving, but I also wanted us to heal and somehow be a happy family again.

One weekend the two of us got up early and drove a long way. Sara said it was six hours. We stopped at a dog-friendly beach park called Bean Hollow in Half Moon Bay. We spent the afternoon playing in the surf. The smell of the salty air and the wind on my face made me think about Julia. She was right; I could still visualize the ocean and the sky when I concentrated. Later, we shared a warm blanket and the contents of her picnic basket, a box of Saltine crackers, some sliced cheese and a couple of roast beef sandwiches. No words were necessary. Sara could see the devotion in my face. And as for me, I fully understood that this constant friendship was what she needed.

Ashlundt was tied up all weekend at his new clinic, so we stopped at a motel that allowed dogs on the way home. It was called the Puppy Pound. Nothing fancy, but the room smelled like lemons, and the bed sheets were warm to the touch, probably fresh from the dryer. Sara sat quietly, watching some Adam Sandler movie on the Pay-Per-View. She couldn't bring herself to laugh even once. I lay on the bed next to her the whole time. In some ways, this reminded me of how I used to crawl into bed with some of the hospital patients. Only Sara's hurt was so very different than the boy with the broken legs, or the lady with MS. What she needed was to be loved on the simplest level. She slept with her arms wrapped around me that night. I don't think she watched even one minute of the various tear-jerker movies that kept coming on the television in the room. Yet, when I woke up, there were rumpled tissues everywhere and empty boxes of Kleenex scattered about. I stepped over them on our way out of the room.

Back at home, Sara started looking for new activities to fill her empty time. She ran out to OfficeMax one afternoon and returned with what she told me was a heavy journal. For hours, she would sit on the edge of her mattress - or on the glider chair in what had been, and always would be, Colson's bedroom – writing in it. Sara's pen rolled smoothly against the pages. I often wondered exactly what she was writing, though I had a pretty good sense of the overall theme. Sometimes, she would stop to take a break. She'd reach down for me, wrap her arms around my neck and weep. I never left her side in those months after Colson's passing. We were partners in agony with no end in sight.

****

The turnaround began on a warm Sunday morning, some ninety evening meals after the accident. Sara and I were in the backyard. I was digging holes in the dirt. Sara was planting some seeds in the garden when Corky caught us by surprise.

"Hey, Sara. Hi, Luke. What are you guys planting? Anything colorful?"

"Oh, hi, Corky." I heard Sara rub her hands together, wiping off the soil. "Just a few morning glory packets. That and some tulip bulbs that one of Ash's patients gave us."

"They'll be pretty there. I've just planted a full bed of Creeping Myrtle on the bank behind our patio. It's going to be a purple haze of glory when it takes hold."

"That sounds really pretty. How's Tim?"

"Tim's his same old loveable self. Misses you and Ash, though. Luke, too. So do I." She reached down and gave me a hug and tweaked my ears.

"I know, Corky. I'm sorry."

I heard the creak of the lawn chair as Corky sat in it and took a deep breath.

"Listen, Sara, I know we haven't really talked much since the accident. But look, no matter what happened, you're still here. I'm still your friend. Ash still loves you. And of course, so does Luke."

I barked twice to verify Corky's observation. Then I heard Corky stand and step closer to Sara and continue her motivational speech.

"Look, you need to start pulling your life together; stop blaming yourself for Colson's death. You know it wasn't your fault. So do I."

Sara dropped a small shovel in the dirt and sighed softly. "But it was my fault, Corky. I took a phone call. Didn't pay enough attention... I..." Her jittery voice tailed off.

"No! You were a great mother to that little boy. Listen, it was an accident. You're a strong woman. For God's sake, you beat cancer! I've read your book. You have so much to share with other people." Corky stepped closer. I could almost feel her put a hand on Sara's shoulder. "Remember how you told me that being a therapy dog and helping others would help Luke through his blindness?"

Sara sniffed quickly. "Yes, Corky, I remember."

"Well, don't you think that helping others will get you through this? Think about it, Sara. Why not start healing yourself by helping others? That's the motto that's gotten you by until now."

Sara was quiet for a minute. I heard her sniff a few times, then it sounded as if she stood and embraced her friend.

"I know you're right, Corky. Thanks for always being a straight shooter."

Their hug went on for a long time. It sounded as if they were both crying. Then, they walked around to the front of the house while I sat and hoped that Sara would be inspired enough to restart her life. It was difficult for me to watch her clinging to her past when she had so much to give others. She had to forgive herself and move on. It was the only way.

After Corky left, Sara came back around and finished her plantings. I heard her patting the ground, then washing her hands with the garden hose. I sauntered over for a nice long drink from it. She wiped her hands on a towel, then cleaned my face with it. She shut the faucet, then headed to the house. "Come on, boy." I found my way through the dog door and followed her into Colson's room where she sat writing in her journal. I had just decided to take a nap when she blurted out, "Luke, you know something? Corky's right. I'm gonna do something. I just don't know what it is yet. But it's true. We can't just go on moping like this all the time."

She spent the next few days sitting in Colson's room on the glider writing in her journal. I was becoming somewhat bored with napping when she announced, "If I'm gonna help other people like Corky suggests, I need to get out in front of them." Then she went back to writing.

We went for a walk in the woods again the following day. The air was full of spring. I sniffed from one plant to the next, peeing on as many as possible. I hoped that like spring, new beginnings would start to evolve for Sara.

To amuse myself, I started to pace my walk to match the crunch of her shoes on the pebbles and twigs. The air was warm, and I could hear a mother bird squawking in the trees at some intruder who must have been invading her nesting space. At that moment, Sara said the words that I knew would help her.

"I'm going to develop a speaking business based on my book, Luke. It just feels right."

I barked my approval, and, this time, instead of sitting on a log and crying she yelled, "Come on, boy! Let's get back to the house."

She sat in her office for days on her computer. She was typing away with a renewed purpose. It reminded me of the days when she was turning her thesis into a book. I loved the sound of her fingers pressing away on the buttons.

Ashlundt strolled into her office one late afternoon and plopped down in the easy chair next to her desk. "What're you working on so hot and heavy?"

"A marketing plan." She offered no further response.

"A marketing plan for what?"

"A speaking tour based on my book." The typing stopped.

"Really? Won't that mean a lot of travel?" I heard him shifting in his chair.

"Yes, but you're never home, so you won't miss me." Her voice was full of tension.

"Why would you say that, Sara?" He sounded alarmed.

"Because it's true, Ash. You're busy building your new business. I'm going to do the same."

I heard her nails on the keyboard typing fast and furiously again. Ashlundt stepped quietly out of the room.

****

One morning, as we sat in her office about 30 evening meals later, she called her publisher at John Wiley and Sons in Hoboken, New Jersey, and asked for Claire Dennis.

"Claire, it's Sara. Did you get the marketing plan for the speaking tour based on my book?" She shuffled some papers on her desk. "You did? Good. Have you looked at it? What do you think?"

I was frustrated because, unlike Ashlundt, Sara never used a speaker phone. I couldn't hear what Claire was saying on the other end.

"You do? That's great. Yes, yes… I agree. A tour will help me get through it. Thirteen cities? You really think it might lead to more? A year? Wow."

I could feel that Sara was on her feet now dancing around. I became excited too. I started to wag my tail in her delight.

"The morning shows? You think with the world the way it is that people will relate? Claire, this is fantastic. Yes, I know it'll be a lot of work. You want to have a working call to hammer out the details? Tomorrow? What time? Yes, that works for me. Talk to you then! And thanks."

She hung up the phone and exclaimed, "I've done it, Luke! I'm going on the speaking circuit! I'm going to start helping others again."

She flipped on some upbeat music on the radio that she kept on her desk and continued to dance, picking up my front feet and hopping around the room. I stood on my hind legs and did my best to keep up with her. My heart soared. I hadn't sensed her to be this happy since our little one left us.

The next morning, Sara's phone rang early. She raced to her office to take the call. I followed close behind.

"Oh, hey Claire. Thanks for getting back to me so quickly. Wow. Details of the first trip already… Three days in Chicago?

When? That soon. Wow, I'd better put on my roller skates; get ready."

I could hear her typing on her computer furiously.

"The following week in New York? Five days?"

She finished responding to all the details, then began to run frantically around the house. I could hear her going through her closet in her bedroom pulling out clothes and evaluating her wardrobe.

"Hmmm, no this won't do. This one's so outdated. Good Lord, Luke! I'm going to need to go shopping. I haven't kept my clothes up-to-date enough to be out in front of people."

By that night, she had an entire checklist she was running through – shopping, packing, perfecting her speeches, grocery shopping for Ashlundt and me, making a hair appointment, getting her nails done. She discussed it with me numerous times.

That evening, she ordered Chinese from a local takeout and waited for Ashlundt to come home. He was late as usual, and she'd already eaten her half of the vegetable rolls and shrimp with spicy Chinese greens. I got a few scraps in my bowl as well. I loved spicy food.

"Sorry I'm late, Sara. What's that? Looks good." He plopped down on a kitchen chair and started scraping food out of the takeout boxes onto a paper plate. I started to drool at the thought of it.

"Ash, I've done it. I'm going out on a speaking tour."

He was silent for a moment, then said, "Congratulations." His tone was unenthusiastic.

"Well, I guess you don't need to get too excited about it."

"Why would I be excited, Sara? You'll be gone a lot, won't you?" Now he was sarcastic, even as he chewed his meal.

The air was filled with tension.

"What does that matter? You're never home. When you are, you're working or sleeping. It's not like we have much of a life these days."

"Hey, that's not fair. I'm building a business. I've been trying to do the best I can under the circumstances."

"Yes, it is fair. You haven't touched me, showed any affection since…" her voice trailed off.

I heard Ashlundt spoon some more food in his mouth. "I've just been tired, Sara. That's all. It's not about you. It's about…" He grew quiet and took a swallow of water from his glass.

"Ash, it's more than that. You blame me. Don't you? You are taking it out on me because of the accident."

I heard him shove the plate away from him and scoot back his chair as if to rise from it. "I'm not going to get into this right now. I'm exhausted. Been a hard day."

She quickly changed the subject. "Don't go. I need to talk to you about Luke."

"What about Luke?" Ashlundt sat upright and pulled his chair a little closer to the table.

"It's important that you really take care of Luke while I'm gone. He's very self-sufficient around the house and the yard. But I assume you'll feed him his meals?"

"Of course, I will! Why would you think I'd let him go hungry?" Ashlundt reached down and touched me on the head.

"Well, you've all but ignored him since he got his PRA diagnosis. What's with that?"

"It's… nothing! You just took over, and I let you." He sounded defensive. "You wanted to be the one to help him. I was rebuilding my business and our lives."

"Well, now I'm asking you to share his care with me. When I'm gone, he needs to depend on you. Will you take him to the office with you, or leave him here at the house?" Her voice was full of accusation.

"It depends on my schedule, but I'll look after him; don't worry." He whispered the last words. "I can ask Tim and Corky to watch him when I'm tied up. They love his company."

"And you don't?"

He sensed her sarcasm. "You know that's not true." Ashlundt stood up abruptly and left the kitchen without a reply.

I heard a deep sigh from Sara as she cleaned up after him. I didn't think Ashlundt would neglect me, but I was probably going to look forward to long visits with Tim and Corky with Ashlundt's busy schedule. If only Ashlundt exhibited more warmth toward me and Sara… maybe she wouldn't have had to go away from us.

****

And so it was. Sara's speaking tour began. She was gone for seven to ten evening meals per trip. The house grew terribly lonely. But I knew it was best for Sara to get her life back on track again.

The first day Sara was gone, Ashlundt called Tim and Corky. As always he used the speaker phone.

"Hi, Corky. It's Ash. Listen, as you know, Sara's traveling this week. My hours have been crazy at the clinic. Could Luke stay with you for the next few days?"

"Of course he can. We'd love to have him." Corky sounded excited.

"Great! I'll bring over his kibble and one of his beds. Just for a few days."

I enjoyed my time with the Bensons. It involved lots of treats, and they both played jingle ball with me, even though my heart wasn't in it anymore since the accident. That sound of the bell was a cruel reminder of a prelude to disaster.

Ashlundt picked me up three evening meals later. I followed him home and tried to make myself small and unnoticeable by going into the master bedroom and curling up on my bed. I didn't want to be in his way, or make him angry. But, he seemed absorbed on his computer, and the night passed uneventfully. His indifference was familiar, but still hollow.

The next morning I awoke to a sound I hadn't heard in ages. "Luke, come," Ashlundt called from the kitchen. He had filled my bowl with some kibble and leftover bacon and eggs from the frying pan. I raced to him, plopped down in front of my bowl and gobbled it down. He had disappeared into his office when I finished, so I ran to get my ball thinking he might play with me. I dropped it at his feet and waited. "No, Luke. No time to play." I slunk off to the bedroom. Then, another shocker, "Luke, come!" I scrambled to find him in the garage, and he quickly lifted me into his SUV. On the way, he made a call to his office. "Ally, I'm bringing my dog, Luke, with me today. You think you could look after him this afternoon for a while?"

When we arrived, the smell of fresh paint, new carpet and freshly-brewed coffee assaulted my senses. The sound of fingertips tapping computer keyboards and several voices greeted us. The lobby space felt large, and I sniffed a variety of plants around it. I followed his scent into his office and sat while he gave Ally instructions. "You'll need to take him out every few hours so he doesn't have an accident on the rugs. He's quite housebroken, but has no way to get out."

"Of course, Dr. Jaynes." Ally had a nice sounding voice.

"And, I've brought some kibble for you to feed him around five this afternoon. Keep him in your office. I don't want him to get underfoot of the patients."

I could hear the unhappiness in every word he spoke. His determination to succeed with his business was also reflected in his voice. Too busy to worry about me, on subsequent office visits, he usually put me in a back office and had his assistant attend to my needs. Ally was very attentive, but I could tell that I was an additional burden to her already growing workload. Unfortunately, now it seemed that I was just a burden to Ashlundt as well.

****

I was at Tim and Corky's when Sara made her triumphant return from her first trip. I heard her footsteps running up their front steps, a brief knock and then, "I'm back, Luke! Hi, Corky!"

My heart leaped in my chest, and I ran to her voice and jumped to drape my front legs over her small shoulders. "Oh, Luke! I missed you!" She immediately sat down on the rug and gave me a bear hug, laughing and rubbing my head. It was the first ounce of affection I had felt in so long.

"Sara, how was it? Was it great?" I could feel Corky hug her.

"It was amazing, Corky! I keep getting more and more cities added to the tour." She squeezed me again. "People are really responding to my talks."

"Knew you'd be a hit. Want a cup of tea or a glass of wine?" I heard Corky walk to her kitchen.

"Thanks, Corky," Sara called after her, "but I'm gonna make a special dinner tonight. Luke and I need to go to the market. Thanks for taking such good care of my boy. I'll have you two over for dinner while I'm home!"

In the car on the way, she punched in Ashlundt's number and left a voice mail. "Hi, I'm back. Please be home by seven. I'm gonna make us a great dinner. It'll be nice to catch up."

That night she pulled out the red tablecloth, the wine, the candles and set the dining room table, describing each step to me. "I'm making Chateaubriand for two!"

I was hoping she might make it for three. Oh well!

Instead of arriving home at seven, Ashlundt dragged in at eight. "Sorry, I know you've made dinner. Got held up." I heard him kiss her on the cheek.

"That's okay, but it might not be as good as I had hoped since it's been sitting in the oven." I heard her shuffling dishes from the kitchen to the dining room. I positioned myself near Ashlundt's chair to listen to their dinner conversation.

"Well, why didn't you check with me before you started it?"

"How can I check when all I ever get is your voice mail?"

Ashlundt took a few steps toward the dining room. "Sorry, honey. Well, let's eat, right?"

I heard the pouring of wine, then Sara said, "I had some real success in Chicago. Claire's gotten more requests for me. I –"

"That's great." He cut her off. "Food's delicious, Sara. Thanks."

She was silent as they both chewed the meat.

"Do you want to tell me about your day, Ash?"

"I'm sorry, honey. Just too tired to rehash everything. I'm really beat and have to study a file before bed. Mind if we talk later?"

"But, aren't you going to finish your meal, Ash?"

"Of course, it's delicious." I heard the hurried movement of his utensils as he gobbled the rest of his food down quickly.

"There. Finished."

Sara was silent. Then, "Don't you want dessert? I baked us an apple pie."

"No, I'm good. Thanks. Great job on the steak." And with that he was up from the table and into his home office.

I listened intently as Sara slowly finished her meal – alone – then cleaned up the dishes. I followed her from the dining room to the kitchen, expecting to hear her cry, but she was silent throughout the process. This was really bad. If only there was something I could do to bring them together.

****

She was only home for four evening meals before her next trip. I went into the pattern of hanging out in Ally's office at the clinic, or staying with Tim and Corky, and he was right; they did enjoy my company. Delightfully, Corky *cooked people food* for me instead of giving me kibble. Roast chicken. Mashed potatoes. Glazed carrots. Tim loved to play Frisbee with me when he got home from work. It was a special Frisbee with a sonic buzz that I could follow. Tim had bought it just for me. There were times that I stayed with them for days because Ashlundt was too busy with work. I didn't mind; they were my second home. Warm, loving people, they had a good marriage, and I always got a handful of buttery popcorn when they watched TV.

Each time Sara returned, I heard the hope in her voice, so different from the detachment in Ashlundt's tone. After her third trip, she was filled with excitement. She arrived back after dinner and came bounding into the house. I greeted her with barking joy and a tail that couldn't be stilled.

"Luke, my boy! I've missed you so!" And down we went on the rug in the den. She rolled me over on my back and scratched me in the perfect spot on my belly to get my leg going like crazy.

Ashlundt came in from the kitchen with a subdued "hello."

"Ash, people have been so responsive to my talks about unconditional love. It's really been overwhelming. So many great questions I'm getting from audience members and the interviewers."

"I'm happy for you, Sara. That's great news." He sounded encouraging.

"The down side is that my publisher keeps adding more cities to my tour, which means I'll be away longer than I thought."

"Well, that's what you wanted, isn't it?" A sarcastic tone crept back into his voice.

"Uh, I think what I wanted was to help other people. It's like being a therapy dog for Luke. I needed to help heal my pain. Speaking of therapy dog, I've got to get this boy to the hospital while I'm home. Start visiting more patients again."

"And how long will that be this time?" Ashlundt's voice seemed suddenly hopeful.

"A few weeks. Well, I'd better get unpacked. Come on, Luke. You can help me."

And so the pattern continued. Sara would leave. Ashlundt would either take me to the office in someone else's care, or he'd leave me with Tim and Corky. Long periods of time passed, and I longed for the days when Ashlundt, Sara and I were a family. The hole in my heart seemed to stretch wider.

****

It happened one night after Sara's return from another long trip that seemed to be the last of her endless travel. Ashlundt made dinner, set the table, then made Sara a proposition that surprised us both.

"You've been traveling for about a year now, Sara. At least, it's been a year since…" his voice trailed off for a few moments.

Sara sat silently. She was chewing on a freshly baked onion roll.

"I've been thinking," he began again. "The clinic is doing extremely well these days. I'm up to three associates and was thinking of adding a fourth."

"Really? Anyone in particular?" I heard her put down her fork. I imagined that it had a big piece of roast beef on it. It clanged on her plate.

"You," he replied.

"Me? Why?" Her voice was full of doubt and uncertainty, almost bitterness.

"Well, let's see, with your latest appearance on *Good Morning America,* your visibility, and all the other publicity offers that you're receiving… well, you would give the business even better positioning. Let's take advantage of your success and finally combine our efforts."

"And why do you think this would be a benefit for me, Ash?" Her voice sounded oddly frustrated. "I mean, I'm very much in demand right now."

"Well, uh… didn't you always say you wanted us to work together? I mean, being an associate in an established practice will give you even more credibility. And our administrative staff can help you handle a lot of the paperwork and phone calls you have to do yourself now." He's tone seemed to change from confident to pleading.

"So, this is all business-related?" Sara's disappointment was clearly audible.

"Well, of course. What else?"

"I'd thought that you might want me to spend more time at home; be more closely related to what you're doing." The skepticism returned to her voice.

I knew that he just didn't get it when he responded, "Well, uh, that, too."

I heard her push back her chair and stand. "Let me think about it." Her footsteps moved away, and I followed.

Sara retreated to her "crying room." I followed her into the master bath. She had shut the door, but opened it enough for me to squeeze in when she heard me scratching. She then closed it immediately. I could feel her slide down to the floor. Soon she pulled me over to her. "Oh, Lukey. What's happened to us? He's so cold to me. How long does my punishment go on?"

I wondered the same. When would he forgive me for being blind? When would he stop punishing Sara for Colson's death? His self-absorbed manner challenged everything that we had in continuing to love and support him. Every time she left, he would put my care in the hands of others. Every time she came home, he didn't make time to be with her except at dinner. He would always claim that he was exhausted or had more work, leaving us to spend quiet time together. But we kept trying. I always had a wag in my tail for him. I continued to try and get him to play ball, often bringing it to him and putting it at his feet, with only an occasional positive response. If he had given me any indication that he wanted me with him, I would have sprung into action. Every time Sara returned home, her voice was full of hope that he would be different. She often would fix him a nice candlelight dinner, or suggest they go for walks or try to have a conversation with him. I knew she would give anything to be with him, but he continued to be distant.

Now, she sat up on the edge of the bathtub and rubbed my neck. "I have to make a decision, Luke. I can't go on with Ash the way it's been. I love him, but he's broken his promises to me." She scratched my head in thought.

"I can either leave now, or try one last time to make our marriage work. What should I do, boy?"

I pressed into her and whined, licking her ear. I tried willing her to keep trying. Ashlundt needed her now more than ever. This was the true test; to love someone when it was the worst. Ashlundt needed Sara and me to heal the pain of both his past and present. But how?

"If I leave him, Luke, will you still love me and go with me?" She rubbed my head.

I pressed even closer and placed my paw on her knee. She had to keep trying.

"This will be the last time, my friend. But one more try. This is it." Sara wept for quite some time in the bathroom. Eventually, she washed up, sprayed on some perfume and went back to Ashlundt in the kitchen.

I followed, eager to hear her response. As I arrived on the warm brick floor of the kitchen, I was temporarily distracted by the scraping of the plates over the garbage can. Ashlundt was cleaning up from dinner. I strolled by my dish just to make sure he hadn't absent-mindedly scraped something into it, the way he sometimes used to do for me. As luck would have it, he hadn't.

"I'll do that later, Ash. Sit down with me." Sara's tone was serious.

I heard them push back the kitchen chairs. I lay down next to what had always been Ashlundt's chair at the head of the table.

"Here's my counter offer," she began. "You want me to join your practice? I'll come and work with you."

"You will? That's great, Sara!" He sounded pleased.

"Wait, there's more to it." Her voice became stern.

Ashlundt shifted uneasily in his chair. "Okay. What is it?"

"I'll come and work with you *if and only if* you will agree to try and love me again. And Luke, too," she whispered.

He was silent for what seemed like a long time. Finally, he stood up from his chair and drew a deep breath. Then, he sat back down again. "I do love you, Sara."

I felt his hand on my head. He caressed behind my ears.

"And I love Luke too."

"Ash, let's face it. We haven't been a couple since the day Colson died. How are we supposed to continue on like this?"

The room fell silent for a long while. Then, finally, Ashlundt exhaled loudly. "I… I'm sorry, Sara. It's been so hard for me."

"Does that mean you don't think it's been hard for me?" There was pain in her voice. "That I haven't also needed comfort and reassurance?"

"Don't you think I know that? It's just… you were there in the park, and I wasn't. I can't get over the guilt of not being there, Sara." He sobbed a bit as the words left his mouth.

"But, Ash, it wasn't your fault. *I* was there. *I* let him slip through my fingers! I know you blame me!" She uncharacteristically banged her fist on the kitchen table, and I jumped in surprise.

"No, Sara, no. If I had been there, I might have prevented it. It's not that I blame you. I just can't get past… the pain."

"But, will you at least try, Ash? Will you try to reconnect with me, and Luke? Will you open your heart to us? That's all I ask. Everything… our marriage… hinges on it." Her voice was pleading.

I heard him get up from his chair and go to her. "I've been living in fear of losing you. I haven't been… decent to you. But, so bitter that you were gone… gone so much. I'll try, Sara. I'll try. I really wanna make you happy. That's all I ever wanted was for us to be a happy family." He sounded forlorn.

I walked over to them, and Sara knelt down next to me.

"And, Ash, just because Luke is blind doesn't make him any less of a friend. He's such a remarkable dog if you would take the time to watch him." She gently rubbed my head. "He's so self-sufficient in so many ways. Have you ever noticed that no matter how much you ignore him, he's always there to lick your hand or be next to you to offer his devotion?"

Ashundt knelt next to her; I felt both their hands on my head and back.

"Yes… he's a… great dog." I felt his desperation to appease Sara.

"You never talk to him like you did before he was diagnosed with PRA. You never truly pay attention to him. Take him back into your heart. How could you not?"

I felt his large hands rubbing my back like he used to do. My love for him melted into them. If I had been human, I would have cried tears of joy.

"I… I never really… I didn't realize that. But, okay. So maybe it's true. I'll surely try and make things better." Ashlundt's tone was quiet and apologetic.

My heart leaped with gladness that he was willing to try.

Sara stood. Ashlundt rose up next to her.

"Ash, I'm sorry, but I don't believe that you didn't realize." Her voice was accusing. "You have to know that you fell back into your old patterns. What I don't understand is why you were so great with Bear going through his cancer, but you can't be the same with Luke and his blindness. Explain it to me."

I heard him turn and go to the kitchen sink. He moved some dishes around the counter and hesitated for a moment. Sara walked over to him, and I followed her.

"I… can't really explain it." Ashlundt sighed deeply. "I don't think I understand it myself. Maybe because there was a treatment for Bear, but there's none for Luke? I thought I could fix Bear. Luke's blindness is too much like watching my brother linger… and die. I'm so helpless to do anything for him."

"But, that's not true!" Sara's voice rose in protest. "If you'd just *participated* in preparing him for it, you would have seen how much it helped him. You could have been a part of helping him. Don't you see?"

I waited for his answer, afraid to move and distract him from it.

Ashlundt took a deep breath and sighed. "I think it goes back to when you were sick. It was too painful for me to watch you go through it at first. I can't bear to see him blind. It hurts too much."

"Oh, Ash. Can't you get it through your head? It isn't always about *you.*

"I know. I… I mean. What can I do to fix this?" Again his voice was full of desperation and fear.

"Just love us, Ash. Just love us. I want to offer you everything that I am, but you've broken your promises to me. If you want me to stay with you, take Luke and me back into your heart."

I heard him put his arms around her. I joined in and pressed my body against their legs. I felt the immediate response of his hand. Choked sobs racked from his chest. I felt Sara pull him closer into her arms. I prayed this would be the beginning of the healing of our family.

Carol McKibben

Chapter Eleven

The Realization

The following week, Sara and I started accompanying Ashlundt into work every morning. He had named his clinic The Jaynes Institute. It was a short twenty-minute ride east in Woodland Hills. Ashlundt allocated an unused portion of his building to be constructed into a classroom for Sara's workshops.

Ashlundt settled into a routine of focused attention aimed at Sara and me. I felt happier than I had since Colson's death.

Ashlundt knew that his life with Sara hinged on demonstrating his true feelings for us both. I noticed small but important changes almost immediately. One night as they ate dinner in the kitchen, he was intent on how best to lay out her new classroom. "Draw me a sketch of how you want it to be set up, Sara. Where do you want the Smartboard to go? How about a flat screen plasma video screen? Where would you want it? I could hear him push pad and paper toward her. And then he tweaked my ear and gave it a gentle rub. Later, as he dried the last dish from dinner, he offered a fine suggestion. "Hey, let's take Luke for an evening walk. You know, like we used to do."

About 30 evening meals later, Ashlundt introduced Sara at her first workshop.

"Ladies and gentlemen, I'm pleased to present to you the bestselling author and nationally acclaimed expert on the subject of unconditional love. Would you please welcome, Sara Jaynes."

Sara placed me next to her podium in the classroom, and I served as a primary example in her lectures. Apparently she had become quite well-known. Her workshops filled up quickly. That first class, in front of some fifty students, she spoke about how dogs were the best illustration of unconditional love.

"You can hit a dog one minute, and the next he'll lick your hand." I felt Sara kneel next to me as she spoke. "His loyalty is unwavering. A dog doesn't care if you're beautiful or not; a dog will love you whether you are handicapped or whole. When you're angry, a dog will wait patiently. When you're sad or sick, a dog will comfort you. When you leave a dog alone for a day, weeks or even months, he'll greet you with joy and appreciation. A dog doesn't put conditions or boundaries on his love. He doesn't react by turning on you if you forget to care for him. A dog greets you with joy in the morning, or every time you walk through your front door. If a dog can do this, why can't we?"

"But, Mrs. Jaynes," shouted a woman's voice. She sounded so close that she must have been in the front row. "Most people have no idea what unconditional love really is."

"That's right." Sara continued. "That ignorance is reflected in our society with overflowing jails, the high divorce rate, violence in our schools and the increasing incidence of alcohol and drug addiction."

"But why is that?" A man's voice came from further back. "I mean, why don't people know what it is?"

"Because we're programmed away from it in early childhood," Sara walked around and knelt next to me again. "If we did what we were told and were *good* boys and girls, our parents *loved* us. People around us smiled and spoke approvingly to us. But, when we were bad, those signs of approval and *love* disappeared. We were taught by these consistent experiences that love was *conditional.* We learned that we had to *buy love* from the people around us with our words and behavior."

Yet another woman asked, "What's wrong with conditional love? That's the way we were raised. That's how the world works; we see it everywhere; why's that wrong?"

Sara rubbed my head, then stood up. "Let's go back to the 'buying love' concept. Let's suppose you are infatuated with your boyfriend and you propose to pay him a dollar every time that he tells you that he loves you. Let's say that you did that for a month. At the end of that month, would you feel loved?"

I could *feel* everyone nodding their heads side-to-side in unison. "No. Of course not," answered the woman who asked the question.

"That's right," Sara affirmed. "No one can feel loved when it's simply bought and paid for. We only truly feel love when it's given to us freely."

The same man that had spoken before asked, "But, how do we get there? How do we get to real love?"

"Real love is *not* putting your own happiness above that of another person." Sara was moving around the room now. "Real love means caring about another without the thought of what we might get for ourselves. Real love is when we don't put conditions on people in order to love them. It's not real love when other people like us for doing what they want us to do."

Another man's voice then spoke up. "So, when we make mistakes, if they really love us, they shouldn't feel disappointed with us?"

"That's right. Even if you get sick, or even get in their way, they shouldn't feel disappointed with you – that's unconditional love."

"What about if we don't do what other people want?" The same participant persisted.

Sara hesitated for a moment. "Yes... even if someone doesn't behave toward you the way you want. That kind of love has the power to heal us. It can bind us together and create relationships beyond anything we've ever known."

I wagged my tail in approval and barked. Sara's audience laughed and applauded. In that moment, I knew she was thinking of Ashlundt and how she might be putting conditions on him for her to stay with him. She was right to answer in the affirmative. There was no other way to help him, other than showing him how to overcome his issues. Not staying to help would be *not loving* him unconditionally. I hoped that she would practice her convictions to help him.

People began to flock in droves to her lectures of hope. She used stories of how my love for her helped her overcome cancer and get through the loss of her child. I could feel the emotions of the individuals in the audience as they came to grips with the issues that held them back from offering unconditional love to others.

Ashlundt occasionally sat in on her lectures. One night over a meal of Chicken Caesar Salad and garlic bread in the kitchen, he scooted his chair around closer to her and began to question. "Sara, isn't what we have real love?"

I heard her scoot even closer to him. "Ash, do you remember how unbearably empty you felt after we lost Colson? Remember how you let your anger fill you up?"

"Yes." His legs seemed to get a little jittery under the table.

"Tell me why your work became the overwhelming driver in your life at that time?" Sara put down her silverware onto her plate.

I heard him put down his fork. He was silent for a moment. "I think it was because I was trying to fill the emptiness inside me."

I heard her take a bite of salad and chew thoughtfully. "Once you built the clinic and had the respect of the community and your colleagues, did you feel fulfilled, even happy?"

"In the beginning, but not anymore," he replied quietly. His feet were still jittery under the table.

"Do you think it's because anything that you use as a substitute for real love never lasts?"

"But, Sara, everyone around us works to succeed. And, of course they become emotional when something tragic happens." His voice was mixed with frustration and sadness.

I heard Sara move her chair so close that her body was touching his. I felt her place her hand on his nervous leg. "If you loved me unconditionally, would you have pushed me away and filled your life with work to feel better? Or, would you have turned to me for love and comfort?"

"I…" he hesitated and placed nervous hands under the table and squeezed my back.

"So instead of turning to the person you profess to love the most, you're filling your life, your emptiness with work as a substitution for real love?" I heard her push her plate further away from them. "How's it make you feel?"

Ashlundt seemed to fidget even more, this time dropping his napkin on my head underneath him. "Sometimes satisfied.

Mostly frustrated... I should have turned to you, but you were in such pain..."

"Ash, you need to go back to the real source of your anger. Go into some sessions with your mentor therapist." She took a deep breath. "Don't you see the pattern? It's not just me you've pushed away. What about Luke since his diagnosis?" She was quiet for a moment. I could only imagine they were intently staring into each other's eyes. "Please, Ash, for me, please go and see your therapist?"

He was silent for a moment, then drew a deep breath. "Yes. I'll do it. For me. For you. For us both, if it'll make things better. You've stuck with me through everything that's happened. I... I owe you this."

I got up, shook my body, stretched and put my head on Sara's knee, wagging my approval. Sensing that this would be all Ashlundt could absorb in one sitting, I barked and begged for a walk. They both followed me.

Carol McKibben

Chapter Twelve

The Cure

True to his word, Ashlundt began seeing his old mentor. He took me along to the sessions at the home of his old teacher, Dr. Jacob Lubin.

"How do you like retirement, Jacob?" Ashlundt sat down and patted for me to sit near him.

"Hate it, Ash. Bored to tears. I'm really glad to see you. Tell me what's on your mind." The older doctor poured each of them a glass of water, setting them on the coffee table between his leather chair and the large love seat he had offered to Ashlundt.

"I'm apparently not over my old issue of losing my brother." Ashlundt took a sip of water, and I could feel him moving uncomfortably next to me.

"Tell me what's been going on," the elder man asked. He smelled of pipe tobacco and strong tea. "You've had a rough go with your son and all."

"My wife Sara, when I asked her to join my practice, I saw her success as a best-selling author only adding to my own. But I was clueless about her area of expertise." He sipped his water again.

"You mean unconditional love, right?" Jacob picked up something from the side table next to his chair. "I have her book right here. Brilliant. Have you been placing conditions on those you love?"

"Apparently."

"How so?"

"I've behaved… badly. Not only to Sara but to Luke here." Ashlundt scratched the top of my head.

"Go on. What else?" I heard Jacob lean forward and pour more water.

"When Colson…" Ashlundt stopped and was quiet for a moment. "When Colson died, I shut Sara out. "When Luke started going blind, I did the same to him." He scratched my head even harder.

"And were you protecting yourself in some way?"

Ashlundt reached down and wrapped his arms around me, "Yes…" he sighed. "Being so… having no way to save Colson; protect Luke. Sara was there… when Colson died…" he choked on his words.

"And you weren't? You blame yourself – for Aaron, for Colson, for Luke?"

"Yes. Yes. Yes. For all of it. I can't protect them." I felt a shudder run through Ashlundt's body as he clasped me even tighter to him.

"Ash, would you say that you are blocking the pain you feel by building a barrier in between yourself and those you love?" Jacob's voice was filled with wisdom and compassion.

"Yes… I don't want… to lose them!" His voice became almost a whisper. "I'm worried that Sara will leave me if I can't fix this!"

In that moment, I knew how much Ashlundt truly loved us all and how helpless and angry he felt not to be able to prevent anything that had happened. It was the confirmation I was hoping for, but wasn't sure I'd ever hear with such sincerity.

****

The next morning he patted me awake as I slept soundly on my bed in the master bedroom. "Shhh… Luke, let's go." I stood, shook off my sleep and followed him to the garage where he lifted me into the car. We drove to Starbucks with him singing along to *She Loves You, Yeah, Yeah* blasting on the radio. I waited in the backseat while he ran inside. Moments later, the front door swung open and the smell of warm cinnamon bun made my stomach growl. I nosed at the paper bag that contained its heavenly aroma. "Hang on, boy. It'll be all yours in a minute."

I couldn't believe my ears.

We soon pulled into the garage. Ashlundt opened the door for me, and I hopped down and followed him into the kitchen. I could hear him slowly opening the paper bag, then the *plop* of the delicious bun in my bowl. It was devoured before it had time to grow cold. And it wasn't even my birthday!

His footsteps led me back into their bedroom. I had to hear this, so I settled down in my bed.

"Wake up, Sara… wake up… I brought you your favorite. Chai Latte."

I heard her moan and then stretch. "Ash, oooh! Thank you! My hero."

"And, I didn't even get one for myself. That's unconditional, right?"

They both laughed. I went into a fit of rolling on my back and snarking at the air in my bed.

After a moment, they were quiet. I heard him sit on the side of the bed. "Sara, I want to ask your advice about something that's been bothering me."

"Of course, Ash. What's up?" She took a large slurp of her tea.

"It's about my brother, Ardin. I've really not felt comfortable talking about it until now."

"Sure, Ash. What about him?" I heard her kiss Ashlundt on the cheek.

"Well, when Aaron had the accident, I think Ardin blamed me for not getting to him quickly enough. That… he blamed me for Aaron's brain damage and… ultimately, his death."

"Ardin? Really? I've never picked up that vibe from him before. Has he ever had a conversation with you about this?"

I heard the bedcovers rustle and could only imagine that she had pulled him down next to her.

"No, not in so many words. More just the looks he used to give me when Aaron was unconscious. And the way he tries to dictate my life, like I don't have enough sense to be in control of it." His words became muffled as if he'd buried his face in her neck.

"Ash, I had no idea. Hey! You're gonna spill my tea. Give me my neck back for a minute so we can talk this out."

I heard them both giggle like kids.

"Okay, Ash. So maybe you're right. But rather than carrying this around with you, go see Ardin. Talk it out with him. And know that if he *does* blame you, the problem lies within him, and not you. What you may be seeing from Ardin could be just a reflection of your own guilt. Know what I mean?"

Ashlundt sighed. "No, not really. He's always been so judgmental. Tough to please."

"Ash," Sara took a sip of her tea, "You've been carrying around a lot of guilt. What makes you feel that you don't project it onto Ardin?"

"I just think you're reaching on this one, Sara." I heard him go into the master bathroom, wash his face and return to sit beside her on the bed.

"Reaching? Really? I don't think so. Trust me. Go talk to him." I heard her laugh and hit him with a pillow.

"Hey! Watch it!" He laughed back at her and then paused. "Maybe I should talk to him. Thanks. Now come on lazy bones, we need to get ready for work! And, I need a cup of coffee!"

I lay there and felt my heart lift. The closeness they once shared was beginning to return. The tone of their voices was so much sweeter. So much more than just respectful. It actually sounded like affection between two people who cared for each other deeply.

****

Ashlundt took me aside in the backyard the following afternoon. I could tell by the spring in his step that he was up to something good. "Hey, boy. I need your help." He paused by the side bushes and stroked the top of my head. "So, how about you take Sara for a long walk? I want to set up a surprise for her."

I barked three times to let Ashlundt know that I was up to the task. Scooting through the doggie door, I was back inside the house and in Sara's home office in a flash. She was working on something at her desk, so I jumped up and placed my front legs in her lap and began to nudge until she finally gave in.

"Okay, you win. I'll take you out. Just give me a minute to get my sneakers on."

We were out in the woods within minutes, crunching on the fallen leaves. I found the droppings of small animals and investigated. I kept pushing to go further away from the house.

Sara complied, and we whiled away the late afternoon. Ashlundt was busy in the backyard when we returned.

"What's this, Ash? A barbecue? All by yourself?"

"Yes, baby back ribs, corn on the cob, a mixed green salad with blue cheese. And, a filet for Luke! You like?"

"I like!" She laughed and walked to him. I knew they were hugging, then kissing because they were making those happy smooching sounds. I walked around them, wagging my tail, beside myself about the steak to come.

I had heard more laughter between them. Oftentimes I would find the bedroom door locked in the early evening, or awaken to their intimacy in the middle of the night. The first time it happened, I expressed my approval by chasing my tail and barking with joy. I could hear their laughter at my reaction.

Ashlundt awoke with the morning alarm the morning after our backyard barbecue. He quickly hit the off button, then rolled over and patted Sara gently. "Hey, you stay put in bed; get an extra few minutes. I'll take Luke for his morning walk. It's chilly out there."

"You're an angel," she spoke into her pillow as we went into the nippy December morning.

I delighted in the crunch of the gravel under his feet, and his voice guiding me around the trash cans that had been set out the night before. He hummed *She Loves You, Yeah, Yeah, Yeah,* which was quickly becoming his theme song. I could feel a reconnection in his touch on my head.

Our bond grew stronger throughout the morning. As soon as we arrived at work, Ashlundt brought me into his office and guided me to a new bed that he had built for me. I had heard him hammering away in the garage for days. It featured a soft, furry mattress and a wooden step to help me climb in easily. Now, I had two special beds at work, one in each of their offices. I felt very special indeed that Ashlundt was looking after my comforts.

****

The holiday season approached. Ashlundt put up a jingly Christmas tree in the den. It was sad not to see the lights and sparkling ornaments, but I loved the smell of fresh pine. Speaking of wonderful smells, Sara cooked up an assortment of holiday treats in the kitchen. Pumpkin bread, gingerbread cookies and sugar cookies were a few of my favorites.

Four evening meals before what they always called Christmas Eve, Ashlundt started to talk to me again about his practice. I had missed hearing him share the details of his cases and clients. "Business is booming, boy. I've never had so many patients. Hey, I hope to take your Mommy away on a nice vacation soon. Is that okay with you?"

I barked my approval. It was about time they finally got away for some relaxation. After all they'd been through, how could I protest?

We were finally a threesome again. I was included in all his activities – going to the office, attending meetings with him, taking walks together. Ashlundt would bounce his thoughts off me as he had before. "Luke, what do you think about the new client?"

I would cock my head, listening intently, and he would go on.

"The man claims that his work is so stressful that he's gonna have a heart attack. But, what he's experiencing is panic attacks. I need to get to the bottom of it. I'll send him to his physician for a complete workup. Once he gets a clean bill of health, I can get down to what's really happening."

I enjoyed these little one-way conversations. And I loved hearing the friendly, confident tone of Ashlundt's voice. Frankly, I'd missed it.

His other immediate concern was the office environment. Even though Ashlundt's moods were changing, his prior harshness had set the tone for everyone around him. Inter-office personnel disagreements and mistakes plagued him.

"The receptionist is complaining that the secretaries are piling too much of their work on her. My partners think Sara is getting too much visibility over them. Will it never end? Why does this always have to happen over the holidays?"

He occasionally, however, reverted to locking himself in his office to be left alone when the day hadn't gone his way. He still hadn't been able to completely rid himself of the self-doubt and pent-up anger that continued after Colson's death. But, of course, I understood, and he continued to work on it in his weekly sessions with Dr. Lubin.

His progress was slow but significant and took an upward turn the next day in therapy in Dr. Lubin's home office. The older psychologist had made them both a cup of tea, then settled into his chair. "You might have forgiven Luke and Sara, but you haven't forgiven yourself for Colson's death, *or your brother's accident.* You'll never heal until you do, Ash."

"But, Sara and I are back together again; I mean the three of us," he argued.

"Yes, but you *still* haven't forgiven yourself, Ash! Sara tells me you react badly to everyday problems. You still close yourself off once in a while." Dr. Lubin took a sip of his tea. "When your brother had his accident, you blamed yourself because you couldn't get to him in time. You saw it as your fault because he was in the water so long. Then, the long months of his lingering were like agony for you. So now, whenever tragedy strikes, what do you think you do?"

"Well, if I look at it as a therapist from the outside, I think I let my anger over not being able to control the situation *control me.*" He was silent for a moment. I could hear him breathing heavily. "With you I've discovered that I punish those I love for creating the tragedy – I blamed Luke for his blindness and Sara for Colson's death, and, in a way, for her own cancer. I know that I have to forgive myself. Rationally I know that I *didn't* cause my brother's accident. It isn't feasible for me to blame myself for what happened to him. But, I do."

I heard him nervously rubbing his legs through his khaki pants as if they itched.

"Ash, you need to forgive yourself for Aaron's death. Think about it. Could you have possibly gotten to him any sooner?"

He paused and cleared his throat. "No... not really."

"Okay, let's end there. Think about that." The therapist took another sip of tea. "Now, how about a game of chess?"

****

A delicious meal of kibble mixed with left-over tri-tip highlighted my evening at home. Then, the three of us took our usual walk. This time we headed to the Equestrian Center. Sara asked about Ardin. "Ash, you went to San Diego last week. Did you see Ardin?"

"Yep, I saw him." He let out a deep breath.

"And?"

"You were right." Ashlundt slapped the side of his leg. "He doesn't blame me. It's all in my head. He thought I was nuts to think it."

"What about your feeling that he tries to boss you around?"

"Man, I felt just like we were teenagers again when I brought it up." He chuckled to himself. "He messed my hair and punched me in the arm and told me I would always be his younger brother, and to get used to it."

"Good. That's one less thing on your worry plate." Sara paused on the trail. I could hear her arm sliding over his windbreaker. I imagined she was rubbing his arm.

"But how do you see me getting angry over everyday problems? Jacob mentioned that today. Give me one example." This sounded like a challenge.

"That's easy," she replied without contemplation. "Our CPA called me today. She told me that she'd gone over quarterly numbers with you, and that she tried to have a logical discussion about some of the discrepancies she found. Instead, you gave her the third-degree; told her that she had made a mistake; to go back to the drawing board. She was ready to let us go as clients."

"Well, she caught me at a bad time. I'll call and apologize."

They seemed rooted in the same spot with this conversation, so I found a mossy area next to a tree and plopped down for a rest.

"No, that's not the point, Ash. You're a psychologist. What would you tell a patient who behaved in that manner?"

"I would say that there's an underlying cause for that type of behavior."

"Okay, what else," she pressed on.

"I'm obviously not happy with who I am. My self-doubt, it's forcing me to blame other people for my unhappiness and insecurities. Or, at least I think that's what happens sometimes."

I turned in their direction and barked my approval.

"Let go of your doubts. Let your love and concern for others be your objective. It's there inside you. Can't you feel it?"

Ash again grew quiet, perhaps searching for the feeling that Sara was questioning about. Finally, he spoke up. "Yes. I know the feeling. But every time I think about Colson I get so angry. Full of despair. How are we to get past it, Sara? I feel like it'll always be there." Fear crept into his voice.

I heard her sigh deeply. "You'll never get past the sorrow that you feel, Ash. But you can get past the anger if you focus on what I've been telling you. I will always love Colson, but I can't change what happened." She choked back a sob.

It wasn't as if a bell went off, though I could have sworn I heard the echoes of one ringing out. Ashlundt seemed suddenly to understand. "Sara, I've been like a guy carrying it around like baggage in an airport. For sure, that isn't going to make me a productive person. The thing is, I need to decide how I want to experience life going forward. And that's the hardest part of all this."

"Yes. That's right, my love. I struggled so hard after Colson died. I wouldn't go out or see anyone. I just stayed with Luke and cried until I had nothing left." I heard her walk over to a log and sit down. "Then I realized that I had to heal myself. I could close myself off, or I could start caring about everyone around me. That's what the book tour was about."

Ashlundt walked over and sat down next to her.

Sara went on. "I made a conscious decision. What about you? Will you be more forgiving and loving? Or will you continue to give in to anger or sorrow?"

I got up and walked close to them, wanting to feel and not just hear their emotions. Standing next to Ashlundt, I felt him reach for Sara and close the gap between them.

"Obviously I want the first choice, Sara. But my emotions and the stress of the business... sometimes it becomes really overwhelming. Isn't that normal?"

"Of course it's normal. But don't you think that if you forgive yourself it'll be easier for you to overcome the negatives that you encounter every day?" She was silent, then breathed deeply. "You know, Ash, the love inside you becomes the love other people feel," she said softly.

He was quiet for what seemed a long time, then I heard him give her a big squeeze and a loud smacking kiss on the cheek. "Sara, you're amazing, and what you are saying... it feels so... right."

I turned and found Sara's hand and put my head under it, then licked it. She responded by squeezing my ear gently. I knew that she received my quiet approval.

We walked on for a long while with only the sound of the crunch of the equestrian path under their shoes. It made a rhythmic tune that played in my ears. I hoped that Ashlundt would perhaps finally learn from Sara's wisdom. I just wanted them to be happy and to find a way to overcome the darkness of the past.

Chapter Thirteen

The Learning

Things seemed to be getting better, particularly through the holidays.

Anya, Asa, Asmara and even Ardin came for a visit. I had lots of playtime and people food! Sara scolded everyone one evening in the dining room for their generosity toward me. "Hey, Luke's going to get really fat if you people keep giving him table scraps on the sly!" This in the middle of a scrumptious bite of turkey and Russian dressing that Asa had kindly slipped me in the kitchen. Of course, that was after the gravy that Anya had poured over my evening meal. I had almost made a clean getaway with it all when Sara stopped Asmara from handing me a buttered roll as he walked by my dish. Awww! I could smell the golden butter; almost had it on the tip of my tongue.

New Year's came and went. Everything gradually settled back into our normal routine of daily walks and going to the office.

Fourteen evening meals after Ashlundt's family left, my stomach started telling me that maybe I overdid it. I went to bed one night feeling overstuffed and nauseous. The next morning I had a hard time getting out of bed, even after a full night of sleep. The pain in my stomach wouldn't leave me. I pushed through the day but had little appetite that night. This was hardly like me to not want to eat at mealtime. I was totally confused. Maybe I was still stuffed from the extra food I'd been treated to by the family, I guessed.

"Ash, did you notice that Luke left most of his dinner?" Sara rubbed my somewhat rounder belly as we sat on the sofa in the den together.

"He's probably spoiled from all those good holiday meals, Sara." Ashlundt laughed and reached over to pat me on my thigh.

"No, no, it's been too long for that. Hope he's okay. It's not like him to leave his food." She moved closer to me and put my head in her lap. Even though my stomach still ached, I closed my eyes and sighed at her loving touch on my head.

Ashlundt immediately sensed that I was hurting the next morning when he got out of bed. I heard him wake Sara. "Something's wrong. Look at Luke's face – he's in a lot of pain."

I felt Ashlundt kneel down next to me. "His stomach… it's tense and sensitive to my touch. Let get him over to Suzi at the clinic right now."

I felt his strong arms lift me from my bed, and I whimpered a thank you. The extreme pressure of the pain was becoming unbearable. I felt like I was going to burst.

Sara was on her cell phone calling the vet. "Suzi, are you at the clinic yet? No? Can you meet us there? It's Luke. He's in a lot of pain. We think it's his stomach."

I was ushered into the old familiar clinic with its Pine Soil smell and slick tile floors and to the back where I heard Suzi's reassuring voice. "It's okay, boy. We're gonna take some x-rays and blood tests. Probably do a sonogram too."

The tests themselves weren't too terrible. The vet took my temperature and felt around all over me. I could feel her listening to my heart. Plus, Suzi had given me some medicine that kicked in just before the sonogram. I started to feel a little less pressure inside. After the tests, Ashlundt and Sara sat with me on the floor and kept their hands on me as we all waited. Soon, I heard the vet's familiar voice.

"Sara. Ash. Here's what I know so far. There's something weird going on with his liver. I want him to have some more tests to pin it down. If that's all right with you both?"

"Absolutely," Ashlundt stated firmly. "Do whatever you have to so we can get him feeling better."

"He's stable enough right now. I'll need you to take his x-rays and drive him up to Ventura to the Veterinary Surgical Group.

It's an acute care hospital with the latest, most advanced diagnostic equipment. I'll call ahead to Dr. Vandersloan."

"Thank you," Sara uttered softly. "We'll run there right now."

The ride took some time, but I was in less pain than I had been earlier. I was able to nap on my cushion in the back of the SUV. Sara had thoughtfully brought my stuffed bear, and I used him as a pillow.

This new clinic had a funny smell. It reminded me of the day we unpacked Ashlundt's new laptop computer from its box. Sort of like a new-technology smell. There were lots of noises inside the clinic – beeping devices and metallic sounds – that drove me crazy at first but slowly faded into the background as we waited to be seen.

Ashlundt and Sara spent the rest of the day waiting and consulting with the doctors while I went through a battery of tests. I was poked and pinched. Something they gave me made me sleepy. I felt tubes being run up my rear end, and people's voices buzzing around me, but it was hard to pay attention to what they were saying. I was in such a strange haze.

After what seemed a long time, Dr. Vandersloan, the one who had been testing me, brought me into a room with my humans and broke the terrible news.

"I'm sorry, but it appears to be Hemangiosarcoma... an aggressive form of cancer in dogs. It's present in both his spleen and liver."

They had immediately started to rub on me when I entered the room. With the news, I felt my humans' four hands jolt from my back in surprise, then immediately return to try and comfort me.

"The abdominal pain that you first saw this morning was caused by internal bleeding." He stepped forward and patted me on my head. "The bleeding stopped on its own accord, and Luke's condition has stabilized. He's actually continued to improve today. He's doing pretty well right now." I heard him step away from me. "You can take him for a short walk if you'd like. He seems to be in good spirits. I think after such a long day he probably just needs some time with you both."

I had no idea what this could mean for me. Sara took me out for a short walk, while Ashlundt hung back with the vet to talk further. I was so happy to be outside, to breathe in some fresh air after a day of being poked at by doctors. Sara was quiet. But no matter, I was just hoping that Ashlundt could finish his business inside so that we could all jump into our car and go home. I felt sore in all the places they had violated. I longed for my leather sofa with the TV blasting and the voices of my humans laughing together. Instead, when Ashlundt joined her, they were quiet and somber, and I could hear Sara sniffing.

"Don't cry, Sara. We'll get through this. Luke will get through this," he softly comforted her.

Soon, we stopped in a sweet-smelling grassy area, and they dropped down next to me. Sara started petting my back in a soothing gesture. "My sweet boy, how can this be?"

Ashlundt scratched my ears. "Sara, the vet says that this kind of cancer can cause severe internal bleeding at any time without warning. He wants us to leave Luke with them overnight."

"No!" Her voice was filled with alarm.

"Sara, listen to me. They can keep a close eye on him and pump him full of fluids to replace the blood he's lost." I felt his hand on my head. "If he remains stable overnight and there's no more tests to be done, we should be able to take him home sometime tomorrow morning."

I tensed up at the news. In all my days since I was a puppy, I couldn't recall a single night when I slept anywhere other than home, or at the Bensons.

"Oh, Ash, I don't want to leave him all alone here!" Sara cried.

"He won't be alone, honey. He'll be well cared for." His hand left my head, and I could hear him rubbing her leather jacket. "If he starts to bleed in the middle of the night, we won't be able to help him quickly enough. Just trust the vets here, okay?"

"But, they're strangers. Can't we stay with him, Ash?" She was pleading.

"We'd just have to sit in the waiting room all night, Sara. If you want to do that, we can." He sounded committed to whatever would ease her distress.

"But he won't know where we are!"

"Would you feel better if we just get a hotel room close by and come back early to see him in the morning?"

"Y… Yes, please." She blew her nose and sniffled.

I felt the warmth of their hands on my back, but I was afraid for myself for the first time in my life. I didn't want to be separated from them. We had all just truly been reunited, and now this. I didn't know what this meant to our harmony. I dreaded that Ashlundt would reject me again.

They reluctantly left me. A kind woman that the doctor called Amy took me somewhere in the back. She led me to a holding container that had a soft pad, blanket and my Teddy Bear that Sara left for me. A bowl of water was at the front of the container. I was so thirsty and lapped down the water only to vomit it up minutes later.

"Poor, baby," Amy's voice soothed. Then I heard her call out, "Dr. Vandersloan, Luke just threw up his water; do you want him on an IV tonight?"

Soon I felt the container door open, and Amy's voice was comforting. "Here, Luke, I'm just going to stick this into the catheter in your leg; won't hurt. Good boy."

The door soon shut, and I lay there feeling hungry and wondering when they would feed me. I listened to the sounds of metal and the voices of the humans. A strange smell offended my sensitive nose, and my stomach growled as I drifted off to sleep for a while. I tossed and turned most of the time, and my stomach began to hurt again.

They came for me the next morning as promised. Dr. Vandersloan brought me out to a carpeted waiting room. I was overjoyed to smell my humans who immediately hugged me warmly.

"Oh, Lukey boy, we really missed you!" Sara exclaimed while scratching behind my ears.

"The night just wasn't the same without you, boy," Ashlundt whispered, before kissing me on the forehead.

Our happy reunion was harshly interrupted with some more bad news.

"Dr. and Mrs. Jaynes, if I could have your focus for just a moment?" Dr. Vandersloan's tone was stern.

Ashlundt stood up quickly. Sara stayed down in her crouch with me on the floor.

The vet's authoritative voice filled the room. "We just reviewed his CAT scan that we took on Friday. It reveals that no tumors can be seen in other parts of Luke's body. This indicates that the immediate problem is isolated to just his spleen and liver."

"Is that good news?" Ashlundt questioned.

"In some cases, yes, but the real concern here is that Luke continues to bleed out. There's a suspicious mass on his liver. We'd like to do surgery on Sunday morning to remove the spleen and that mass from his liver. The surgery is his best short-term option." The vet's tone was terribly serious.

"What do you mean?" Sara sounded worried and confused.

"Well, there's a slim chance that the tumor is not malignant. It may be just a benign hematoma." I heard him tap his pen on something metal. I assumed it was one of those medical clipboards vets used. "I once removed a 12-pound hematoma from a dog that went on to make a full recovery. But, anyhow, there's no way to know for sure what the tumor really is without removing the suspect tissue and sending it to a lab for analysis."

"There's hope?" Ashlundt's voice sounded strangled by anguish.

"There's always hope, Dr. Jaynes," the vet replied. "To improve Luke's odds of coming through the surgery, we're going to type and match donor blood for him. Having several units of fresh blood immediately available will improve his chances."

"Coming through the surgery?" Sara's voice was almost hysterical. "Do you mean it might *kill* him?"

The vet moved closer to her. "There's always risk with any surgery. But without it, he won't make it."

"Why can't you do the surgery today?" The urgency in Ashlundt's voice was unmistakable.

"I'm sorry, Dr. Jaynes. We already have back-to-back surgeries scheduled this afternoon. I can't get to him until tomorrow morning. Also, we need time to get the fresh donor blood."

I was allowed another walk with my loved ones. I could hear the sadness in their breathing and sullen tones of voice.

"If it's cancer, I don't understand how he could have gotten it, Sara," Ashlundt declared. "We've always taken the best care of him; the best food. I don't know if it could be environmental to our area? First Bear, then you, and now Luke."

I felt exhausted after only a few steps. Maybe that restless night in the clinic had sapped me of my energy. I decided to lie down in the grass alongside the parking lot.

"Let's get him back inside, Ash; he looks worn out," Sara ordered.

Suddenly I felt Ashlundt's arms embrace me. He lifted me to his chest and buried his face in my neck, just as he always had with Sara. And then relief washed over me. I heard the simple words that made all the difference to me.

"I'm here for you, my friend."

I didn't remember much after that. I heard the vet say that I'd been resting comfortably and snoring a lot. I napped often. Time had no meaning for me. I was on what they called "IV fluids" and couldn't measure the passage of time without my evening meals. I remember someone checking on me and speaking to me in a kind voice. "Hey there, big guy. Just gonna fix this here for you." They did something with the IV bag. Later, I recall being rolled along, then going to sleep.

When I awoke, I was okay for a moment. My head felt hazy, but I was sure that I was alert. Then, the soreness kicked in. I felt a muffled burning sensation right in the center of my belly. I heard a woman's voice talking to me. "You're doing well, boy. We hope you can go home Wednesday or Thursday."

I drifted in and out, wondering what had happened. I had no sense of passage of time. And there was no daylight or nighttime inside the clinic. Not that I'd have been able to tell the difference since I'd lost my eyesight.

Eventually, I awoke feeling quite hungry. One of the doctors gave me a small portion of soft meat that smelled like lamb and rice. I gobbled it down and hoped for more. I heard the familiar vet's voice telling another man, "His long-term prognosis is still not good if the tumors are indeed cancerous."

Ashlundt and Sara finally came for me.

"Lukey, how are you sweetie?" Sara's voice was full of concern.

156

"Hiya, boy. How're they treating you here?" Ashlundt's tone seemed to be playful, although I suspected that this was his way of coping with the seriousness of the situation. I still didn't know how long I'd been away from them, but I was overjoyed by their presence. I expressed my joy with pathetic barks that seemed to be muffled. I felt so embarrassed by my inability to be myself. And my belly still burned pretty badly. I wanted to reach down and scratch the sore spot, but it was covered with a big bandage. Even more concerning, someone put a harness around my neck and chest that prevented me from being able to get to my sore spot. I was only able to sit at the counter next to them and listen to them talk to the vet again.

"With chemo, we can expect him to be with us for about six to twelve months before the cancer returns. If the tumors are not cancer at all, then he'll make a full recovery. We'll know more when the lab results come back."

I just couldn't wait to get out of there. Once Ashlundt opened my door for me, I tried to leap into the car but the things they called staples pulled at my stomach. They stopped me dead in my tracks. Even though the pressure from before was gone, the burning pain left my belly on fire.

"Easy, boy," Ashlundt warned. "You're getting better, but don't push it."

On the way home, my humans talked about waiting for lab results and throwing around many words that I didn't understand, like "homeopathic."

"I asked the surgeon if he could tell during the surgery whether or not it's malignant," Ashlundt spoke from behind the wheel. "He said he really couldn't tell just from looking at it."

"The assistant said it would probably be Monday before we get the lab report." Sara was sitting in the passenger's seat, right in front of me. "They know more about these things."

It was so exciting to be back home. Of course, my excitement was muted by the fire in my abdomen. All the familiar terrain - the carpet, the smells, the rooms and my bed – was heaven to me. During my first walk outside with Sara, I sufficiently marked every leaf and flower in my front yard. It was fun, but also exhausting. Soon thereafter, I headed inside for the leather couch in the den and a long nap. Life was once again good.

It was good, that is, until the afternoon following four evening meals later. I was resting on my special bed in Ashlundt's clinic office when he punched in on his speaker phone.

"Dr. Vandersloan on line one for you, Ash," his receptionist stated.

This friendly voice was followed by a familiar, yet somber voice.

"I have some bad news, Dr. Jaynes. The tumors that were removed from Luke are definitely Hemangiosarcoma. It looks like he's going to have an uphill battle."

I could hear Ashlundt take in a sharp breath. "How long does he have?"

"Six months… maybe more if we do chemotherapy. But the prognosis isn't great. I know this must all be really painful to deal with, but…" His voice went silent.

"Okay, I'll speak to you after I've discussed it with Sara," Ashlundt replied. "Thank you for all you've done for us."

Ashlundt said nothing for a few minutes. I could hear him breathing heavily. I heard him stand up and felt him grasp my collar and gently guide me down the hall. I knew from the number of steps and the direction that this was Sara's office. I heard him shut the door. I walked to my bed and snuggled down into it. *He didn't walk away from me this time.*

"It's bad, Sara. He has cancer. We have to decide whether to do the chemo or not."

I heard a sob from her, and then I knew that he had buried his head in her neck because his voice was muffled. "Oh, God, Sara, this could have been you. I'm such a stupid fool!"

"Why, Ash?"

"I wasted so much time punishing you and Luke for something that neither of you could have helped." His voice was filled with pain.

"Ash, you've been letting go and forgiving; you've made so much progress." Sara's tone was reassuring. "Don't put this on yourself." I heard her chair creak from his weight pushing on her. "It's just life, and we *have* to give Luke every chance that we can! You are standing by him now. We'll do the chemo and buy Luke more time. We'll make it the best few months of his life."

158

"We'll do more than that, Sara." His voice grew stoic. "I'm going to look for other alternatives as well."

The love that I felt in that room at that moment made me forget anything that happened in the past. I wagged my tail and rolled over in my bed to show them my appreciation. They both dropped down to the floor and put their heads close to me, and I covered their faces with kisses.

****

Recovery from the surgery wasn't easy. But soon, my energy returned, as did my appetite and playfulness.

Thankfully for me, chemotherapy has less radical effects on dogs than it does on humans. Sara or Ashlundt would take me to the clinic in Ventura for what they called "single-agent doxorubicin," intravenously given every 3 weeks. The vet used a needle connected by a tube that was wrapped in a bandage. I would feel the occasional nausea, and was a bit sluggish after each session, but otherwise I was almost my old self again. At first, I wanted to lick at the wrap that covered my leg, but Sara and Ashlundt explained that I should "leave it." So, I eventually did, with a little bit of snack bribery.

Ashlundt found one piece of encouraging news on the Internet and called Sara into his office to explain it to her. "There's an experimental treatment called apSTAR." He pulled her over to his computer and read to her: "It's the use of a laser combined with a polymer. Experiments have shown improved rate of primary and metastatic tumor regression in laboratory models of tumors."

"Ash, do you want to try something experimental on Luke?" I visualized that she was standing in front of him with her hands on her hips when she questioned his judgment. "What if it's dangerous?"

"Don't worry. I'll call Dr. Vandersloan; find out more about it."

"Ash, I'm so proud of your efforts to help our boy. Thank you." I heard her give him a big smooch, then leave his office. She stopped to give me a huge hug on her way out.

Luckily for me, he put the call on speaker phone as he dialed the vet's office. Ash got through to him on the first try, "Wow, Dr. Vandersloan, I didn't expect to get you this quickly." He proceeded to ask about the experimental treatment.

"Ash, Autologous Patient Specific Tumor Antigen Response is an immune activating laser procedure. It's been shown to induce long-term tumor immunity and increase the rate of primary and metastatic tumor regression. It's a personalized approach to fighting cancer."

"Is Luke a candidate?" I heard him tap his foot nervously on the floor. "My research shows it increases life expectancy and possibly even cures the cancer."

"Unfortunately, no. The procedure was developed, in part, at Oklahoma State University and is now entering field evaluation on a limited basis. But, so far it's only worked on surface tumors and not on animals with Luke's particular form of this cancer."

"Uh, okay. So, this won't work for Luke." Ashlundt's voice was dejected.

"No, Ash, not this one. I promise you, if I had any possible experimental procedures, I'd recommend them for Luke."

Ashlundt quietly thanked the vet and clicked off the speaker phone. I stretched and walked over to him and thoroughly washed his hands.

"It's okay, boy. The chemo's going to work anyway."

Ashlundt persisted in his search for an experimental cure for me, and I was grateful, even if I didn't understand all the medical terms, or the severity of my illness.

****

A few weeks later I was feeling very good. We had gone for a ride in the car, just for me, and I really loved it. Ashlundt even rolled down the window and let the cool breeze blow through my fur. I had eaten my evening meals like I was starving for several days running. And instead of listening to his conversations with the vet, I would take a nice nap next to him in his home office. Apparently, I must have developed a loud snoring habit because Ashlundt would sometimes nudge me with his foot. "Luke, shhh, I can't hear what the vet's saying."

I drifted off again and awoke to the end of a discussion he was having with Sara. "Sorry, baby. He's not a candidate for anything experimental that I've found so far."

"Ash, we just have to keep faith with the chemo at this point."

Again, I could feel the closeness between the two of them. Ashlundt brought me out of my relaxed state with a tempting offer. "Wanna play bell ball, boy?" I was out the doggie door to the back yard in a flash.

My illness and the fear of losing Sara seemed to be the jolt that Ashlundt needed to come to grips with what both she and his therapist had tried to teach him. His entire demeanor was changing. There was gentleness about him that had rarely been present before. His new approach to living gave me such a sense of greater purpose for my own life. I had helped them get through some of the worst times of their lives, and I knew that was why I was sent to them.

Chapter Fourteen

The Revelation

My disease affected everyone around me. The associates and staff at the Jaynes clinic were moved and inspired by Ashlundt and Sara's efforts to save me, and by the obvious changes in their leader.

I picked up on the subtle clues occurring in the office. But, the changes became even more apparent with the preparation of a surprise party for Sara the day after she received her psychology doctorate. The idea for the party came not from Ashlundt, but his associates who had randomly started to brag about Sara's accomplishments instead of expressing petty jealousies. Dr. Ore, the first associate Ashlundt had hired, stepped into the office shortly before the surprise.

"Ash, the secretaries have it worked out to take Sara to lunch so that Sondra can set up the cake and decorations."

"I hope they didn't exclude her from the lunch, Ben." Ashlundt's voice sounded concerned.

"No, no, not at all, Ash. In fact, the staff, without any prodding, worked out an agreement with Sondra on all their workflow. She was so grateful to be treated as part of the team that she volunteered to be the one to stay behind." Dr. Ore walked closer to Ashlundt. "I love how everyone is really starting to listen to each other and be a productive team."

I heard Ashlundt slap Ben Ore on the back, "Me, too, Ben, me too."

Sara went out to lunch with part of the staff as arranged. Instead of having Sondra handle all the logistics by herself,

Ashlundt, Ben Ore and the other associates jumped in to help. "Here, Sondra," Ben insisted, "let me hang that sign for you. When she went to finish the decorations and bring out the cake, Drs. Breen and Newman immediately offered to help. There was a kindness in their voices that I hadn't heard before to each other. I'd noticed earlier that instead of talking *at* each other they started *listening* to what others had to say. It made me feel all proud inside.

When Sara and the secretaries returned from lunch, everyone was waiting for her with a loud "Surprise!" I sat proudly next to Ashlundt. I could hear Sara laughing and thanking everyone. I heard a cork pop and something bubbly being poured into glasses. "A toast," Dr. Newman offered, "to *Doctor* Sara Jaynes, one of the most valuable assets to this clinic! Congratulations on this wonderful milestone, Sara!"

"Here! Here!" Everyone joined in.

"I… I don't know what to say. You've all been so incredibly supportive. Not just about my doctorate…" she trailed off for a second.

Ben Ore chimed in. "No, Sara, thank you and Ashlundt for showing us how we should treat and respect everyone… especially our most precious friends."

I felt Ashlundt's hand on my head.

"Actually Ben, I shouldn't be in that equation at all… it's all Sara and Luke. Thank you, my love… for showing me the way." He knelt quickly and folded me in his arms and gave me a huge scratch on the head. "Thank you, my friend."

Then, I heard him walk to Sara. "I'm so proud of you. Congratulations!"

I gave the room my most adorable open-mouthed smile, tongue and all.

****

Sara and I went over to visit with Corky one evening while Ashlundt and Tim went to shoot hoops at the gym with friends.

"So, how's my Lukey?" Corky greeted us at the door and gave me a squeeze.

"He's doing great," Sara responded as we followed Corky into her kitchen to the smell of fresh peanut butter cookies baking in the oven.

"What's your pleasure? Coffee? Tea? Wine? Soda?" Corky was the consummate host. She immediately set down a plate with two warm cookies on it for me. I didn't need to be invited. I just wolfed them down quickly. Delicious.

"Oh, he's going to get so spoiled and fat." Sara laughed.

"Let him enjoy it; he's the best and deserves it. Wine?"

"Sure." Sara laughed again. I'll take one of those cookies too."

I heard her sip her wine and take a bite of cookie.

"I'm glad I have you to myself, Corky. Want to run an idea by you."

"Hit me with it."

"Well, I have an idea for a new book, and an accompanying class on how to handle loved ones who are sick and dying. It's based on my bread and butter: giving unconditional love, of course."

"Ooh! Sounds like something very useful, Sara. An extension of your earlier lecture series."

"Yeah, I want to show people that we are all connected; we are not alone but are one together."

"You go, Girl! Amazing how resourceful you can be." Corky hugged Sara, and I could hear the smile in her voice. "What does Ash think about it?"

"Haven't told him yet. I have another idea about it, but I want to run it by him first." Her voice was full of mischief.

"Well, tell me the rest when you can. Now, come on, help me finish fixing these cookies."

****

We were in the conference room at a staff meeting the next day. The associates were sharing problematic cases with Ashlundt. I sat in the corner listening to the various cases and challenges they each faced.

Dr. Newman presented the case of a thirty-five year old woman who was experiencing Monophobia, an acute fear of being alone and having to cope without a specific person in close proximity. "Her closeness extends to having someone in the same house and is part of the agoraphobic cluster." Dr. Newman got up and began to pace around the conference table.

"It's only our fears of being alone that hold us back from truly knowing that we are not alone," Sara offered. "Your patient has an extreme sensitivity to this, but it's truly a part of all of us."

A heated discussion about how to treat the patient followed, but my mind wandered off. I thought about how that really applied to Ashlundt in so many ways. I like to think that I played a small part in helping him to know that he wasn't alone. Whenever Sara spoke, I wagged my tail to continue to be her inspiration.

The three of us sat during the lunch break that day in Ashlundt's office. Sara decided to bring up her book idea to him. They were eating turkey sandwiches on whole wheat – I could even smell the mayo on Sara's and the mustard on Ashlundt's. I ravenously chewed on a rawhide bone.

"Don't you see, Ash, this life is merely a place for us to learn about what is truly important." She mumbled excitedly with her mouth full of sandwich. "We're really all here to help each other. But, people just get so self-absorbed in their fears, and things like guilt and envy."

Ashlundt's chair creaked as he leaned back in it. I heard him move his Styrofoam sandwich box and take a sip of Diet Coke. "Yes, so you've taught me."

"Luke's been such an inspiration. I think his story of how he helped us will make others truly see what's important. I didn't have the experiences with him for my first book. But I do for this one."

"Hard to argue with that. Between you and Luke, I think I may finally have gotten my priorities straight. You have my blessing as if you need it." He chuckled.

I could hear him wiping his hands, a sure sign he had finished his sandwich. I thought about trying to investigate for turkey scraps, or bread crumbs but kept still, eager to hear more.

"Actually, I think we need to write the book together, Ash. We've lived the process of finding true love… our journey to find it… and we need to write and tell it together. What do you think?" I could hear her lean forward expectantly.

"Does this mean that you think I've made it through to giving unconditional love, Sara?" I could hear the hope in his voice.

"That's a strong affirmative, Ash. You've come so far."

I heard him leap from his chair and pick her up in a hug accompanied by laughter.

"Does this mean we're okay? Our marriage, I mean?"

Sara giggled. "We're more than okay, Ash. We're great."

I knew he was kissing her, and I wagged my tail furiously.

Then, he sighed. "But, I'm not the writer that you are, Sara."

I heard them both sit back down.

"You don't have to do the actual writing, silly. We can have brainstorming sessions. You can help me flesh out my thoughts."

"But, I hardly have time to get through my day without adding a book to my plate." His protest was half-hearted.

"Ash. This is important. We need to tell our story. Won't you please help me?"

He was silent for a moment. I could hear them both breathing. Then, he took a deep breath. "You're right. I'll do it, Sara. It'll be Luke's legacy."

In that moment, I knew that my journey was complete. Something told me that it was time for… *something else.*

****

It happened a few evening meals later. I began to experience sharp pain in my belly again. We had gone for a long walk up to the equestrian center before dinner. It was summer. A warm breeze had caressed our faces. I could smell the scent of honeysuckle in the air. When the first wave hit me, I yelped in surprise and staggered to the side of the path. Sara and Ashlundt were in a deep conversation and didn't notice. I had lagged behind them. I did my best to gather my strength. I made it back to the house, immediately retreated to the master bedroom and crawled into my bed rolling with the pain.

Sara's voice called me to the kitchen. "Luke, come on boy, dinner!"

I was hungry but knew I couldn't eat. "Luke, where are you? Come! Dinner!"

I tried to get up but couldn't. Soon I felt Sara's gentle hand on my head. "Ash, come quick; it's Luke!"

I felt him next to me instantly, his hand on my stomach. "Yes, he's in pain again. Damn! I thought... I thought we had more time. This is too soon. Let's get him to Ventura."

While they ran frantically through the house, turning off the oven and gathering their things, I gathered my strength and slowly rose from my bed. I quietly staggered through the house, wishing I could see it all once more. I stopped at my beloved leather sofa. It was as far as I could go.

"Luke," Ashlundt's voice called, "Where'd you go?" Soon he was next to me, lifting me in his strong arms and burying his face in my neck. "Oh, Luke. I'm so sorry."

He carried me to the SUV, and we went to the hospital once more. Sara sat with me in the backseat, holding me the whole way. I could feel her hands trembling and smelled fear in her perspiration. I knew it was a Friday. Ashlundt and Sara had talked about plans for the weekend on our walk. I heard the tears in their voices as my humans gently handed me off to the clinic staff.

After initial tests – some painful poking around my belly – Dr. Vandersloan, who happened to be on duty that evening, asked Ashlundt and Sara to come back to one of the treatment rooms. I was lying on an exam table and felt more comfortable. The vet said, "Luke most likely is bleeding internally again." He placed his hand on my side. "I've given him an injection to help him relax and stop his spasms. We're going to put him on fluids."

I felt Ashlundt and Sara's hands on me as I drifted off to sleep.

Later, they attached me to those tubes again, the one's they called IV fluids. "This should help stabilize him for now," a nurse told Sara, who continued with Ashlundt to stay with me. I drifted off to sleep thinking that the spicy cologne that the vet was wearing was at war with the medicinal smells of the hospital.

I woke up hours later in good spirits but somewhat weak. Ashlundt and Sara had stayed at the clinic during the night and took me home to enjoy the nice weather in our front yard. Tim and Corky came over to visit. Corky brought my favorite sausages and a jar of relish. My appetite hadn't fully returned, but I was still able to devour the treat in just a few bites. People food always beat whatever they had been putting in my bowl all these years. I was content.

After supper, Corky sat down beside me on the patio, wrapped her big arms around me and sobbed like a little girl. Tim knelt beside me, patted my head and told me what a "good doggie" I was. I knew that this would be the last time I would see them. My heart ached. I love them both, and they had been good friends to me.

It was early in the morning when they decided to take me for a nice long walk around the yard. I remembered what our friend, Julia, had told me in the hospital about smelling every flower petal. I rolled in the grass and could smell the soil. The air felt warm on my skin. I made my way slowly around to the backyard to try and sniff out any bones I might have buried and forgotten. I found a few spots but just nosed them. I didn't have the energy to do much else. I feebly lifted my leg on all my old special spots, then I stopped and took in the smell of it all. The trees swayed slightly in the breeze. I knew it was time. I was ready.

They were silent when they helped me into the car for that last great journey. I firmly gripped my beloved bear in my teeth for comfort. Sara brought a little blanket with us, and she used it to cover me in the car like she used to do with Colson when he was tiny. They drove me back out to the hospital in Ventura, where I received a battery of tests including an ultrasound.

Afterwards, Dr. Vandersloan brought them back to the treatment room where I rested on a metal table. "He's bleeding out internally… most likely the result of a ruptured tumor on his liver."

"Please," Sara interjected, "please help him." She broke down sobbing.

"Is there nothing you can do?" Ashlundt questioned.

The vet's voice was grim. "Let me see how he does this afternoon.

They put me in a holding container large enough for me to stretch out. It had a soft pad and a warm blanket, and someone had put my Teddy Bear in it for me. "You rest now, boy," a gentle voice said as he shut the door on the container. I heard the vet tell Ashlundt and Sara to come back at three o'clock.

When they returned, I felt worse. I drifted in and out, my strength draining away from me. We were again in the treatment room, and I rested on an exam table. The paper sheet below me rumpled with my every movement.

"He's deteriorated to the point where we'll have to begin giving him blood transfusions to sustain him," Dr. Vandersloan advised.

"No more." Ashlundt placed his hands on my head in protest. "We've decided that he's been through enough with the surgery in January. Then the months of chemo. We don't want him to suffer through any more treatments."

"You've made a wise decision." The doctor's voice became lower and softer. "Anything we do from here is only prolonging his suffering." I felt the vet's hand on my back, and then he left us.

Sara and Ashlundt spent the next few very pleasant hours just hanging out with me outside. The smell of the flowers and the grass in front of the clinic, combined with the soft breeze of a wonderful summer day, was intoxicating. My appetite came back enough, and Sara fed me a nice big meal of steak and potatoes that she had brought in a foil container. With a full tummy, I laid down for a nap in the grass under a shady tree. I felt happy. I was at peace and so relaxed.

I could hear Ashlundt's voice. "Thank you, Luke... for all that you have taught me, for all that you have meant to us. For teaching me how to truly love... to understand what really matters." His voice broke, then continued. "Thank you for showing me that I never have to be alone again. I owe you so much."

"You will always be in our hearts, boy," Sara sobbed.

I felt the vet kneel next to me. I was so grateful that I didn't have to go back inside the hospital, but would be allowed to remain outside to the end. I heard his soothing voice.

"Okay, boy, just a little stick here. This will make him very sleepy. Once that takes effect in a few minutes, I'll administer the drug to stop his heart. He won't feel a thing."

Ashlundt and Sara wrapped their arms around me. I could feel their tears on my face. I felt so sleepy, drifted in and out, wishing I could tell them how much I loved them. I tried to wag my tail but all my strength had vanished.

"Now, I'm administering the final drug." He patted me softly on my rump. "He seems serene, completely unaware."

It was a Saturday in the early evening, but suddenly the sky became so bright with white light. I could *see* Ashlundt and Sara's faces once again. The vet was still talking to them. I could feel their arms wrap more tightly around me, but the light seemed to surround me. It seemed to have wings that enfolded me.

Then, a new voice. Like music and full of joy and laughter. "It's time, Luke. You are finished here. Ashlundt and Sara will carry your message. A message of unconditional love to thousands of others."

I recognized the voice immediately. It was Julia.

"I promised I'd be waiting for you at the Rainbow Bridge, Luke. It's a special place just for animals to wait for the humans they love. There are meadows and hills for as far as your eyes can see."

I could feel the smile on her face. Its warmth surrounded me. And then it dawned on me; she said *as far as I could see.*

"That's right," Julia continued, "those who have been ill, hurt or old are restored to health and youth here. Your sight will be restored, Luke, just as mine has. I can finally see what a beauty you are." A thrill ran through my soul at the thought of seeing again.

I felt her white-light arms enfold me once again as she whispered to me. "Not only will you run and play with others, but you will have all the food, water and sunshine that you want. You will be happy here until those you love join you. Colson is here, too, and he can't wait to play with you again." I could hear the boy's giggling laughter, and my heart leaped with joy.

It was suddenly so clear that I was sent to Ashlundt and Sara to help her to heal him. Now, they will help others. It is done, and I can leave them until it is their time to join me.

Yet, another thought seemed willed upon me. *Could I go back to help others?*

"Yes, Luke," Julia whispered, "In another form if you so choose. All of us can if we want to achieve a higher purpose."

The white light makes everything so clear. As I am lifted so gently from Luke, the dog, I know that henceforward I must share the gift of unconditional love with all to whom I am sent. Love without conditions will open all the possibilities of the universe. I believe it with all my heart. People will change the world if they do too.

The End

Luke's Tale

Dear Reader,

I truly believe that couples today give up on their relationships because they place unrealistic 'conditions' on each other. But, no matter if you are sick, tired, unemployed, had a bad day or are even angry, your dog will love you. That's why I made Luke, the Dog, the narrator of this story. I want people to see what it means to stick by those they love, no matter how bad it gets.

Life is full of ups and downs, and it's important for people to understand how to ride through the *downs* and why not placing our own expectations on others will strengthen any relationship.
This may seem too out there, but this message came to me in a dream. That and my blind dog, Luke, were the inspiration for this novel.

If I have touched you, please let me know by visiting my Web site, www.carolmckibben.com, and leave me a message. I would also appreciate your honest review posted on Amazon. I'd love your thoughts and reviews!

Sincerely,

Carol McKibben

www.ingramcontent.com/pod-product-compliance
Lightning Source LLC
Chambersburg PA
CBHW061136200626
46817CB00016B/1692